Julian is on the run. He doesn't know who's after him, but he knows he'll have to do something about it. The fact that he's just met his mate makes everything more complicated, especially since Tali has known for much longer than he has and hasn't told him.

Tali doesn't want to have to choose between Julian and the council assassins. One is his mate, the other his family. Since Julian's on the run, Tali knows he'll end up leaving, and Tali won't be able to go with him.

But maybe Julian doesn't have to go. Maybe he can accept the assassins' help and work with them to find out who's hunting him and do something about it.

It's either that or be killed, and Julian isn't about to allow that to happen.

This book is a work of fiction. Names, characters, places, and incidents either are products of the author's imagination or are used fictitiously. Any resemblance to actual events or locales or persons, living or dead, is entirely coincidental.

Julian
Copyright © 2020 Catherine Lievens
ISBN: 978-1-4874-3098-6
Cover art by Angela Waters

Published by eXtasy Books Inc or
Devine Destinies, an imprint of eXtasy Books Inc

Look for us online at:
www.eXtasybooks.com or www.devinedestinies.com

JULIAN
COUNCIL ASSASSINS 11

BY

CATHERINE LIEVENS

CHAPTER ONE

Julian looked around, his hands on his hips. The warehouse was a mess after the attack, and it hurt to see it. He hadn't been staying here long, but everyone had made him feel welcome, and he would miss this place. He didn't know what was next for him—he was with the assassins for protection, but now he *wanted* to stay with them.

No one would be staying in the warehouse, though. They couldn't, not when someone had found it. It had been attacked, and it wasn't safe anymore. That meant they had to find a new place to stay, and since Julian wasn't part of the assassins or a mate, he didn't know what would happen to him.

Well, he *was* a mate, but not of one of the assassins. He was Tali's mate, and Tali was one of the Nix who worked in the infirmary. Julian didn't know if that would be enough for the assassins to allow him to stay indefinitely, but he hoped so, even though he knew they'd always choose Tali over him.

He wanted to help the assassins find out who did this and take them out. He wanted to have a chance with Tali, even though he didn't understand why his mate was keeping him at arm's length. More importantly, he didn't want to be alone anymore. He also had to be safe, which wouldn't happen until he found out who was after him and why.

He supposed he could survive on his own. He had for a long time, and he was more than capable. The fact that he didn't *want* to be on his own anymore was important, though. Now he could get in trouble, and someone would come to help him.

Maybe.

He still wasn't sure what most of the assassins thought of him, but he supposed he was lucky they weren't kicking him out.

"What are you doing standing there?" Roark asked him as he passed by him.

"I'm not sure. I guess I was looking at the damage."

Roark rolled his eyes and straightened an armchair. "There's no reason for you to look at the damage. Go to your bedroom and grab whatever you need. It's why we're here."

It was, but it looked like Roark had trouble doing what he'd just told Julian to do. He was moving furniture, picking up things, and looking around as if his heart had been torn out of his chest.

He'd lived here a lot longer than Julian. He'd been an assassin, and now he was in charge of them. This was his home. Seeing it destroyed, knowing that people had invaded it, had to hurt.

Julian wanted to help, but he didn't know how. He and Roark weren't friends—far from it. Julian had been angry at Roark for killing one of the people Julian had been hired to kill, which meant he hadn't been paid for it and he'd had to listen to his handler yell at him. Julian had wanted to kill Roark for the slight, but he hadn't been able to. He'd tried a few times, but instead of killing him, he'd found himself fascinated by the way Roark and the others interacted. He'd never thought that an assassin could have friends, not the way Roark did. The assassins worked together, of course, but they were also family, and it had made Julian's heart ache.

It still did.

He wasn't part of the assassins or their family. Now that the warehouse was gone, he would have to find a motel or go to his family. He didn't want to pull his family into it, but it would be better than being on his own. Of course, the people after him might be able to find him there, which meant his family would be in danger, too. They were more than able to deal with it, but Julian didn't want them to have to. He didn't want them to know he'd failed.

"How are you doing?" Roark asked gruffly.

Julian blinked at him. "I'm fine." Julian hadn't been hurt, but he was confused. Over only a few hours, the warehouse had been attacked, he'd fought against the attackers, he'd been shimmered to Gillham, where one of the council members lived, and he'd found out that Tali was his mate. It would be confusing for anyone, and Julian's mind was reeling, even days later. He had to accept there wasn't much he could do to help the assassins, even though they'd helped him, and it didn't go down well. "Better than some people," he added.

Roark nodded curtly. "You helped us. Thank you. I don't know if Tony and the others would have made it out of the infirmary in one piece if you hadn't been there for them."

Julian looked away. He rubbed the back of his neck, wondering how to take Roark's words. "I didn't do anything anyone else wouldn't have done," he finally said.

"I don't know if that's true, but still. Thank you."

"I guess I'm going to go grab my stuff. I'll be out of your hair soon."

He moved toward the stairs, but Roark caught his arm. "You'll be out of my hair?"

"You have to focus on your family, and I'm not part of it." Not yet, maybe not ever. It depended on Tali, and Julian hadn't had time to talk to him yet. "I can find a motel or something. I'll let you know if anything happens to me, but you shouldn't worry too much. I'm not your problem. I'll be fine."

The glare Roark aimed at Julian made Julian's step falter. "What do you mean, you're not my problem?"

"I'm not a council assassin."

"So? You worked with us. You helped Tony and the others

out of the infirmary. I know that without you, things could have gone badly for them. That means that you *are* part of the family, no matter what you think. You're not going anywhere, Julian. You're with us now, so you'll be staying either in Gillham or with some of the others, depending on where we find space for everyone. And once we have a new place to stay, you'll be coming with us." He paused. "As long as you want that, too. I won't force you. I know you're in trouble and we're not equipped to help you at the moment, but we'll figure it out. You can count on that. You helped us, and we're going to help you."

"You already helped me. You allowed me to stay here. It was more than I deserved after what I did." Julian had followed Roark and his friends to a cabin in the mountains and slashed their tires. He'd tried to ruin their Halloween party, too, until he'd realized that they were organizing the party for kids in a shelter.

He was an asshole.

He still wasn't sure why he'd turned to Roark and the assassins when he'd been in trouble except for the fact that he knew they could help him. He didn't even know who was after him, and it had been hard to ask the assassins for help, especially Roark. He'd expected to be kicked out, but instead, they'd taken him in. They hadn't even taken much time to think about it.

Julian had never realized how close the assassins were. Now that he did, he was amazed by the fact that they'd allowed him to become part of it. He wasn't family quite yet, but he was somewhat part of it, just like Roark had said.

He cleared his throat. "Thank you. I know it would be much easier for you to ask me to leave."

"We won't abandon you, so stop worrying about it. We never leave anyone behind."

"The people after me could find out where I am and bring

trouble to Gillham. I don't want that to happen."

Roark patted Julian's shoulder, almost knocking him onto his knees. "Don't worry about that, either. If they look for trouble, they'll find it. But we need to rebuild, and in the meantime, we have to be careful. We were all lucky to be able to make it out alive, and I know we'll find a place for everyone while we get the new warehouse in shape, but that doesn't mean someone won't discover where we are and try to take advantage of it. You'll be staying in Gillham with Rocco and the others who were with you when you shimmered there. Keep an eye on them. Rocco can defend himself, but Tony is still healing, and Tali and Jolyn, well, they're not fighters."

"Will you be there, too?"

"I will, but I'm only one man, and I need to have eyes everywhere, just in case."

Julian nodded. "I'll be your eyes, then." Because there was no way Julian would allow anyone to hurt his mate, whether or not Tali ever wanted him.

The warehouse was a disaster, and it hurt Tali's heart to see. It had been his home for so long. Tali didn't know what he would do now, but he hated losing this place, even though he knew the council was already working on another warehouse.

It wouldn't be the same. His room was his safe haven, a place where he could be alone and rest, where no one would bother him. Now, he had to live in Gillham, at least for a while. He'd be safe there, but he'd miss everyone who was staying elsewhere, as well as having his own permanent room.

"I hate what they did to the house," Tali's brother said.

"I hate it, too. There's nothing we can do about it, though."

"I wish there was. It's not fair."

Tali didn't mention that nothing was fair in this situation. Jolyn wasn't thinking straight, which was understandable.

What the assassins did wasn't fair, either, not from some people's point of view. Tali didn't agree, but still, he had to admit that the assassins were complicated to deal with, mentally and emotionally.

They killed people. There was no way around that, and he'd learned to live with it a long time ago. He knew they only killed the people they were ordered to kill, but that didn't stop him from wondering what would happen if one of the council members wanted someone killed for their personal gain. They could come to the assassins and order them to, but would the assassins follow those orders? So far, the council was working for shifters and humanity. They'd only ordered the assassins to kill people who deserved it, people who were hurting other people. That might not always be the case, though, and Tali didn't know what would happen then.

He shouldn't be thinking about that right now. The only thing he should be thinking about was going to his bedroom and packing his things. It was the last time he'd see the warehouse, and he had to ignore the pain in his chest and focus on the fact that soon they'd all have a new home, and that they would be together again.

The assassins were his family, and he already missed those who wouldn't be staying in Gillham.

He and Jolyn headed upstairs. Luckily for them, the people who had attacked the warehouse hadn't gotten that far, so the bedrooms were intact and they had a lot of things to move. They'd been told to grab only the indispensable, but Tali knew no one wanted to lose their things. It was already hard enough that they were losing their home. It would take more than a small bag for him to feel comfortable leaving.

But they had orders. He and Jolyn weren't assassins, but they had to follow them anyway. That meant that Tali would

put all his things in suitcases and leave them on his bed. Then
he would go to Gillham with only his backpack. Someone else
would pick up the suitcases and take them to the new warehouse, and he wouldn't see them for a while.

It felt weird. They were only things, but they were his. He
didn't want to leave them behind, even though he knew he
didn't have a choice.

They made their way along the hallway, and one of the
bedroom doors opened. Tali swallowed when he realized it
was Julian's. He didn't look up when Julian stepped into the
hallway, but he knew what Julian was doing. He was hyper-
aware of his mate, and there was no way to avoid him.

Julian hesitated. He paused, looking at Tali until Tali hurried after Jolyn. He was grateful Julian wasn't saying anything, but he knew he would hear about it as soon as they
were alone.

"Jolyn," Julian said as they reached him.

"Hi, Julian. You grabbed your stuff?"

"I don't have as much as you guys do, but yes. Let me
know if you need any help."

"That's very nice of you. Thank you."

When Tali crossed paths with Julian, Julian raised a hand,
effectively stopping him even though he wasn't touching
him. "I just want to talk to you," he murmured.

Tali didn't know what to do. Julian was his mate. He'd
known that since the first time he'd seen him, even when Julian hadn't realized it. He hadn't said anything, though. Julian
wasn't a council assassin. He was a normal shifter, even
though he was a professional killer like them. He didn't belong with them, no matter how much Tali wished he did.

But he was only here because he was seeking protection,
and as soon as he could, he would leave. Tali wanted his mate,
but he couldn't leave the assassins, not even to be with Julian.
They were his family just as much as his twin brother was.

They'd welcomed him when he thought he only had his brother.

Tali and Jolyn had been in a lab. They'd been experimented on, just like nearly everyone else in the house. Even though he and Jolyn didn't end up having strange powers like the assassins did, they'd still been scarred by what had been done to them, and becoming part of the council assassins, even if only as healers, had saved them. Tali and Jolyn talked about it often enough that Tali was sure Jolyn felt the same way.

Being part of the assassins was empowering, even though they'd never been sent on a mission and they never would be. They were here to take care of the assassins when they came back from missions, and that was fine with Tali. He didn't want to do anything more. He didn't want to hurt people.

But it was still his home. He couldn't imagine not sharing it with the assassins. He hoped to grow old with them and still be a family. Maybe things would go differently. Maybe some of the assassins would decide they wanted to retire like Roark had and they would leave, but in the meantime, Tali wasn't going anywhere.

Julian was, though. He wasn't part of the family, and he didn't have a reason to stay beyond the fact that he wanted to be safe.

"Please, just let me talk to you," Julian begged. "I promise I won't force you to do anything. I'm not that kind of person."

Tali shook his head. "I can't. Not now." He hoped Julian would understand. Just like everyone else, he was in shock at what had happened, but he couldn't deal with anything else right now, especially not with Julian. He wanted to give Julian what he needed, but he couldn't.

Julian dropped his hand. He looked defeated, and Tali yearned to reach for him. Instead, he stayed right where he was and waited.

Julian rubbed his face. He looked tired, but then they all

were. "Fine. I'll give you space. I would *really* like to talk to you, though. We can't ignore this, Tali. We're mates, whatever you think about it. If you're going to reject me, I need you to tell me."

Tali opened his mouth to do just that, but he couldn't.

He didn't want to reject Julian. The only reason they couldn't be together was that Julian would leave, while Tali couldn't. But Tali wanted nothing more than to press into Julian's arms, have Julian curl himself around him and protect him from the world. It wasn't possible, though, so instead of doing that, Tali swallowed and nodded.

"You'll give me a chance to explain, then?" Julian asked.

"Explain what?" Tali couldn't help but ask.

"Whatever your problem with me is. If I know, I can try to fix it."

Tali started to answer.

Julian shook his head. "No. I understand. Go pack your stuff. I'm not going anywhere."

For now, Tali couldn't help but think.

Julian wanted to push, but he shouldn't. He had no idea why his mate didn't want to talk to him, but he did know that now wasn't the right moment to ask for more. Everything was a mess for Julian. He could only imagine how much worse it might be for Tali. He'd been living in the warehouse for a long time, and seeing it destroyed had to be hard on him. Julian didn't want to make it even harder, so instead of doing what he wanted and dragging Tali into a room so they could talk, he went back downstairs.

He didn't want to leave the warehouse, not when his mate was upstairs, but he also knew he probably shouldn't stick around. People would start wondering what he was doing there since he'd already packed all his stuff. So instead of staying in the living room, he headed down to the infirmary.

Rocco had come with Julian and a few others that morning, intent on cleaning up the infirmary and gathering everything that had survived and could be useful. He was working alone, since the twins were upstairs, and Julian suspected he might need some help.

Rocco looked up when Julian pushed open the infirmary door. He was tense, but he relaxed when he saw who it was. Julian wasn't surprised. Everyone was tense after what had happened, and especially so when they visited the warehouse. They probably expected a second attack, and knowing what he did, Julian wouldn't be surprised. A lot of people had it out for the council assassins, especially now that they'd found out the government was experimenting on shifters.

"What are you doing here?" Rocco asked.

"I thought I could help you. I didn't have much to pack."

"Don't you want to get some rest instead?"

Julian shook his head. "I'm fine. Just tell me what to do." Because every time he stopped moving, his thoughts drifted either to Tali and why he didn't want to talk to Julian, or to what was next for Julian.

No matter what Roark had said, Julian couldn't help but wonder if he really would be as welcome in the new warehouse the assassins were building as he had been in this one. He wasn't part of them. He would never be a council assassin, not when he didn't have what it took to be one.

Council assassins had special powers. He was pretty sure that at least a few of them would give them up right away if it meant they could forget what they'd been through in the labs, but they couldn't. It made them special, and it gave them an edge when it came to their job. Those powers made it possible for them to get to the targets and kill them way more easily than it would have been for Julian.

Julian had always been envious of them. He'd wanted to

be a council assassin, but now that he knew why he couldn't, he understood better. It was a sign of honor to work for the council, but after what everyone had been through, Julian realized none of them cared much about that. They wanted to be useful and get revenge on the people who had hurt them, but they didn't care about the honor or even the money.

Julian didn't either, not really. Not anymore. Now that he knew what being a council assassin meant, he still wanted to be one, but that mostly was because he wanted to be part of their family.

He had his own family — both his parents and a brother and a sister. Being a professional assassin was a family tradition, and Julian's brother Sam was the only one who wasn't doing that kind of job. They would be able to help with whoever was hunting Julian, but he still wasn't sure he should bring his troubles to them. They would kick his ass if they found out he hadn't, but still. The assassins were better equipped to help him. He knew that, and his family would realize it if he talked to them. That didn't mean they wouldn't be angry, but hopefully, they would understand.

He really didn't want to get his ass kicked.

"You can start packing those things over there," Rocco said, tilting his chin toward a bunch of stuff he'd piled on one of the beds.

Julian nodded and looked around. He'd fought in this room. There was still blood on the wall from where Rocco had managed to hit one of the guys attacking them with a scalpel. That was how Julian and the others had found out what Rocco's special power was, and Julian was in awe. He didn't say anything about it, though. He knew Rocco wasn't comfortable with it, even though he didn't know why, and he wasn't going to push.

"Do I have to be careful with how I pack them?"

"Not too much, no. Just push everything into a bag."

Julian went to work. The silence was soothing, but he couldn't help but be hyper-vigilant. He doubted the warehouse would be attacked a second time, but that was a possibility they all had to keep in mind. Now that people knew where the warehouse was, they might sell that address to someone else, or even attack again. They'd lost a lot of people in the attack because the assassins were good at their job, but that didn't mean they didn't have a lot more still available.

"What's going on between you and Tali?" Rocco asked.

Julian blinked, wondering where that question had come from. "I don't know what you're talking about." He wasn't going to tell Rocco he and Tali were mates, not when he didn't know whether or not Tali would be okay with that.

Rocco snorted. "That's bullshit. It's obvious something's going on, but since you don't want to talk about it, I won't push. It's your secret to keep, I guess. I just hope he won't continue to be as distracted as he's been lately."

Julian paused as he was pushing a box into one of the bags. "He's been distracted?"

"Ever since you moved in with us."

Dammit. Julian should have realized that sooner. Tali was a Nix, so of course he'd known Julian was his mate from the first time he'd seen him. He hadn't said anything to Julian, though, and Julian wondered if he would have kept that secret if Julian hadn't been close enough to him to smell him. Would he ever have told Julian about their bond? Why hadn't he told Julian when he'd found out?

It could be something Julian had done, but he doubted it. He hadn't been around the assassins long enough. It could be the way he'd behaved when it came to Roark before he'd moved in with them. He'd wanted to kill Roark for taking his targets, but he hadn't put that much effort into it. Otherwise he might have been able to hurt Roark, at the very least. He hadn't, though. Instead, he'd spent time watching Roark and the others and wishing he could be part of their group.

And now he was—kind of.

"I know him better than you do," Rocco continued. "I don't know what's going on, but whatever it is, the circumstances aren't the best."

"I realize that." Did everyone think Julian was an idiot?

"You need to give him time."

"I haven't been pushing him, if that's what you're asking. I wouldn't."

"I know. You're not a bad person, Julian. But you're not one of us, either, and there are some things you don't know and can't understand."

Julian wished those words didn't hurt, but he couldn't deny they did. "I know I'm not one of you. You don't have to remind me." His voice was a little too harsh, but he didn't regret it.

"That's not what I meant. I didn't want to hurt you. But you haven't been with us for a long time, and you don't know Tali's personal history. You also don't know what it means to be one of us. You will learn, but it's going to take time, and you have to open up to Tali. You have to show him you're not going anywhere."

Julian frowned. "You think that's why he hasn't been talking to me? Because he thinks I'm going to leave?"

"What would you think in his place? You're not one of us. You're here because you asked for help, and it was granted to you. That doesn't mean you're going to stay, though. I wasn't sure you would, and I'm still not. What's going to happen once we find out who's after you and we get rid of them?"

Julian hadn't thought about that, either. "I don't know. I want to stay, but I might not be allowed to."

"Exactly. Think about that. Ask questions. Make decisions. Tali wants certainty, and I don't blame him after everything he's been through. He's part of our family, but you aren't, not yet. You're going to have to make decisions about that and other things."

Julian already had.

"You need to talk to him," Jolyn said.

Tali ignored him, focusing on pushing his things into the suitcases. He hoped the two he owned would be enough to move all this stuff, but he couldn't be sure. When had he accumulated so many things?

"Are you listening to me?" Jolyn asked. He put a hand on his suitcase and closed it. "Come on, Tali. We're brothers. You can talk to me."

Tali sighed. "I heard you, and I don't want to talk to him." That was a lie, and he was pretty sure his brother knew it.

"That's not true. He's your mate. Why wouldn't you want to?"

"Being mates doesn't mean we have to be together," Tali pointed out. He looked around, wondering if he could start filling the other suitcase. Or would Jolyn stop him to talk?

"I don't understand why you're behaving this way."

"He's going to leave, Jolyn. Why would I want to talk to him when he's not staying?"

Jolyn crossed his arms over his chest. "How do you know he's leaving?"

"Why would he stay? He doesn't belong with us. He's not a council assassin."

"That doesn't mean he doesn't want to stay, though. How can you know if you haven't talked to him?" Jolyn huffed. "You're infuriating. You're making assumptions, and I don't like it."

"Maybe, but you're not me. You can't force me to talk to Julian."

"But if you don't even give him a chance and get to know

him, how will you know what he wants? How will you know what he's ready to give you? You're his mate. I'm pretty sure he's going to want to stick around if that's what you want, too."

Tali looked away. Jolyn wasn't wrong. No matter how much he tried to keep in mind that Julian was going to leave eventually, there was a part of him that hoped he wouldn't.

Everyone knew how impressed Julian was with the assassins. He wanted to be one, but he couldn't be because he didn't have any special powers. That was something that linked the council assassins to each other — they'd been in a lab. They'd been tortured and experimented on. They'd come out of it with special powers most of them wish they didn't have. Still, they used them, and it made their job easier. It kept them safe. That wouldn't be the case for Julian, though, and it was one of the reasons he couldn't be a council assassin.

Tali suspected that if given a chance, Julian would stick around. It was obvious he loved living with them, and it gave Tali hope. He didn't know if he should foster that hope, and he didn't want to think about it now.

He still needed to talk to Julian, though.

He didn't know when he would be able to make that happen. He and his brother were going to stay in Gillham, and he was pretty sure Julian had been offered the same, but it didn't mean he would accept. If Julian wasn't staying in Gillham, there would be no way for Tali to talk to him. He could call, of course, but this conversation wasn't one that should be done over the phone.

That meant he had to catch Julian here before they left.

He dropped what he was holding in his suitcase and moved toward the door.

"Where are you going?" Julian asked.

Tali looked at his brother over his shoulder. "I'm going to do what you want me to do. I'm going to talk to Julian."

15

Jolyn beamed. "I'll finish packing for you. Don't worry about a thing that isn't Julian."

Tali was pretty sure that wasn't possible, but he nodded and headed out.

He couldn't know whether or not Julian was still around, but he hoped so. His heart raced as he went downstairs, looking around. "Have you seen Julian?" he asked Roark as he passed by him.

Roark blinked at him as if he couldn't quite understand what Tali was asking. "I think I saw him go downstairs. Maybe he went to help Rocco. Why?"

Tali shook his head and headed toward the stairs.

Julian was there, too. He was standing on the landing, carrying boxes and bags of stuff Rocco was packing in the infirmary. He looked at Tali when he heard him, and his eyes widened. He took a step back as if he thought Tali was afraid of him, and Tali felt guilty.

He was the one who'd done that. He was the one who hadn't wanted to talk to Julian, and who'd put distance between them.

Tali shuffled his feet. He couldn't face Julian, but he still had to.

"Did you need Rocco? I can call him," Julian said. "Or you can go to him. He's in the infirmary. I'll stay here for a bit."

Tali shook his head. "I want to talk to you, actually." His heart felt like it was about to jump out of his chest, and he resisted the urge to press a hand against it.

Julian seemed pleased. "I'd like to talk to you, too." He hesitated and looked around. "This probably isn't the best place to do it, though."

"You're right." Tali should have thought about that, but he wasn't sure he'd have another chance to talk to Julian. "I just wasn't sure where you were going to stay, and I wanted you to know that I wanted to talk."

"I'm staying in Gillham. That's where you're saying, too, right?"

"It is."

"How about we meet once we're back there, then? It's probably going to take a while to settle down and put all of this stuff away, but as soon as I'm free, I'll find you."

"I'll have to help Rocco with this. Maybe you can help, too?" Now that Tali had made the decision to talk to Julian, he couldn't seem to move away from him. He wanted to be with his mate. He wanted to spend time with him—to find out what made him laugh and what made him sad. He wanted to shield him from the world and the people after him.

He was rushing ahead, though. Before any of that could happen, they had to talk about what the future would be like for them if they decided to be together. He couldn't allow his heart to get broken, not when it was barely held together with tape and friendship.

"We can talk sometime in the next few days," Julian said.

Tali wondered if it was a way for him to avoid the conversation.

Julian seemed to be reading his mind, and he smiled. "Trust me. There's nothing I want more than to talk to you. Everything is a mess right now, though. We have to settle in Gillham, and I should make sure no one followed me there." He grimaced. "I promise we'll talk, but I don't want to rush into this. You're here because you thought you wouldn't have another chance to see me, but now you know you will. Take your time wrapping your mind around everything. I'm not going to push you."

Tali wasn't sure what he'd done to deserve a man like Julian, and he had to resist the urge to reach for him and kiss him.

Maybe he *should* kiss him, although not on the lips. He

17

didn't want to start anything, and he didn't want to distract Julian, who was looking around as if he expected someone to attack. It was a distinct possibility, and Tali knew they both needed to get back to work.

He moved closer to Julian and kissed his cheek. When he leaned back, Julian's eyes were wide, but he was smiling.

"We can talk in Gillham," Tali agreed.

Julian nodded. "That's good." He hesitated. "But I do have something to tell you now."

Tali froze, wondering what was going to happen.

"I'm not going anywhere," Julian said. "Not now, and not ever if I have anything to say about it."

Tali stared at him. He didn't know how Julian had realized that was his problem, but he was glad he had. This way, he was sure his mate wasn't leaving, at least for now. It gave him peace of heart and mind and the ability to focus on what he was supposed to do—which was finish packing.

CHAPTER TWO

Julian was acting like a creep. Since he was giving Tali space, he should *actually* give it to him instead of standing outside the infirmary where Tali was working and watching him through the windows. He knew that, yet he wasn't about to stop.

He leaned against a tree, watching as Tali moved around the infirmary. He was working with Sei, one of the Nix healers who was based in Gillham. Tali seemed to like Sei, and he was learning a lot. Julian knew it was a good thing, and the smile on Tali's face made him want to go in there and kiss him.

He didn't.

He and Tali had decided they would talk soon, but he wanted to give Tali the time to get used to everything that was happening. Julian's world had been turned upside down, and he could only imagine how much harder this was for Tali. Julian was used to this kind of situation, although nothing as bad as the warehouse being attacked. Tali, on the other hand, wasn't. He might work for the council assassins, but he was a healer. He didn't leave the warehouse often, and never to go on a mission. He wasn't usually faced with the world and the people who wanted to hurt him, but this time, he couldn't avoid it.

Julian sighed. He didn't want to wait much longer to talk to Tali. Yes, he wanted Tali to relax and feel better, and more importantly, to feel like he could tell Julian the truth, whatever that truth was. But Julian couldn't wait forever, not when

19

he didn't know what was going to happen tomorrow. For now, Julian was living in Gillham, and so was Tali. Eventually, though, Julian suspected he was going to have to move. He was lucky the people after him hadn't found him yet, although he supposed that wasn't surprising, considering the warehouse security was high. He wasn't there anymore, though, and eventually, they would manage to get to him. He had to know what was happening when they did. He had to know whether or not he should give Tali more time, or if he should give up and go.

He wanted to stay, yet at the same time, he didn't want to. He didn't want to put Tali, the assassins, or the pack in danger. They were probably more than able to protect themselves, but the pack was dealing with a lot right now, and it wasn't fair to ask them for protection.

Julian's phone rang, startling him. He jerked to a stop as Tali turned around, probably having heard the ringing. Julian didn't try to hide himself. Instead, he raised a hand and waved it at his mate. Tali looked hesitant, but he waved back, and Julian beamed at him. He had no idea what was going on in Tali's head, but he was going to find out sooner than later.

He took his phone out, surprised to see it was Beck. "Hey." Beck wasn't staying in Gillham, so Julian hadn't seen him in a while. They'd never been close, though. Julian hadn't had the time to become close to any of the assassins or other people who lived in the warehouse. He was friendly with them, but he didn't have friends, not exactly.

"Julian?" Beck asked.

"Yes. You were looking for me?"

Beck chuckled warmly. "I was. I have news for you."

Julian straightened. "Is it about the people after me?"

"It is. I think I found out who they are."

"I'm listening." Julian's stomach churned. He was about to find out who was trying to kill him, and once he knew, he could do something about it. *Probably.*

"Does the name Luciano Clemente mean anything to you?" Beck asked.

Julian frowned. "I killed a target once. His name was Giovanni Clemente."

"Same family."

Julian leaned back against the tree and closed his eyes. "They want revenge."

"I suppose. I can't tell you that, but I know they're the ones after you. They were in the same places you told me you were attacked, and apparently, one of them had a hit on you. You have assassins gunning for you, although from what I can see, they're mostly human. I don't think Luciano Clemente knows that you're a shifter."

"Not surprising. I don't advertise that I am."

"That's good. That means he thinks you're human and probably easier to kill. What do you want me to do with this information?"

Julian didn't know. He wasn't surprised to find out it was the Family, as they were called in New York, but he didn't know how to deal with them. He was a professional killer. That meant he snuck inside places, killed his target, and got out. He didn't fight entire families, and he didn't kill anyone he wasn't supposed to kill.

He couldn't stay in Gillham. He couldn't put the pack at risk. He didn't know how powerful the family was, but if they found out that he was here, they would send someone to get him. "What do you think I should do?" he asked Beck.

"I'm not sure," Beck said, sounding surprised. "You should probably talk with Roark about it, though."

"And probably the Gillham pack alpha," Julian added.

His gaze moved to the window again. Tali wasn't looking at him, but he peeked up every so often. Julian wanted to smile and let Tali know everything was okay, but everything *wasn't* okay.

"I've texted Roark. If you tell me where you are, I can send him your way."

There was no way Julian was doing this with Tali so close. "Tell me where he is. I'll join him."

"The enforcers' building in pack territory. You know where it is?"

"I do."

"Wait. He texted me that he wants you to meet him at the alpha's house. Bran will be there, too, as well as Kam. You can talk to the three of them."

Julian had no doubt that if Win had been in the area, he would have been there, too. He and his mate were hunkering somewhere else, though, so Julian would have to make do with Roark.

He didn't mind. He might have hated Roark at one point, but he'd always known it wasn't real hate. He'd been annoyed about losing a job, and he wanted Roark to pay, but he'd been shit at it. He was happy about that, too. He didn't want to hurt Roark or anyone he wasn't paid to kill and who didn't deserve it. "I'll be there soon."

"I'll tell him. And, Julian?"

"Yes?"

"I know you're worried, but you're not alone anymore. You have us."

Julian's mouth went dry. He wasn't sure whether or not what Beck was saying was the truth, but he wanted to believe it. "Thank you."

"Stay safe."

They hung up, and after one last glance at Tali, Julian headed toward the alpha house. He knew where it was, and he was relieved to find it easily. He'd gotten lost in the forest a few times, and while it hadn't been bad, since he actually enjoyed being here, he could do without that today.

A young man opened the door when he knocked. "You're here to see my father?" he asked.

Julian nodded. "If he's the pack alpha, yes. I'm Julian."

The man nodded. "Huritt. Dad's in the office. He's not alone, but I'm guessing he'll want to talk to you anyway?"

"I think they're there for me, so yes."

"I'll show you the way."

Julian followed Huritt inside the house. He still didn't know what to do, but he was relieved he wouldn't have to make the decision on his own. Like Beck had said, he wasn't alone. He didn't know whether or not he would be allowed to stay, and he didn't know if staying would be the right thing to do even if he were, but he didn't have to do this on his own.

By the time he went home that evening, Tali hadn't seen Julian again. He wasn't too worried — they were all trying to find their temporary place in the pack, and for some, like Julian, it was harder. Tali and Jolyn had it easy because they knew where they belonged, but Julian didn't. He'd been walking around for days, exploring the territory and watching Tali a lot.

Tali hadn't known what to think about it in the beginning, but he didn't mind. He liked knowing that his mate wasn't far, and he knew they needed to talk. For the first time, he *wanted* to talk to Julian.

Julian had said he wasn't going anywhere. It gave Tali hope, and now that he had it, he wanted to see if he was right. He wanted to see if he and Julian could have something together.

He and Jolyn stepped into the house. They were sharing it with Rocco, Cam, Dasha, Ox, Roark, and Noel. Noel had been bitching because he couldn't go to the office, but Roark had forbidden him to. It was dangerous, especially with people having invaded the warehouse and possibly having recognized a few of them. They all needed to be careful, and that included Noel. He might be a lawyer, but that didn't mean he was invincible.

The house was new, but it was also soothingly familiar to be with everyone. Tali missed the others, but eventually, he would see them again. The new warehouse was being worked on, and even though it would take time, it would be their new home.

"Hey," Dasha said as he looked up from his phone when he heard the front door. Tali could see him through the open living room door. He looked worried, which made Tali worry in turn.

"Hi. Is something going on?" Tali prayed that wasn't the case because he didn't know if he could face anything more.

Dasha looked around, then got up from the couch. "Has Julian talked to you?"

Tali frowned. "No. Why? What's going on?" He didn't want to freak out, but he could feel the beginning of panic building in his chest. "Is Julian okay?"

"He is." Dasha bit his lower lip. "I shouldn't be telling you this. He should, but I'm not sure he will, and I think you should know."

"Just say it." Tali's mouth was dry, and he wanted to know what was going on.

"Beck found who was after him. It's a powerful crime family from New York."

The bottom of Tali's stomach felt like it dropped to his feet. "Where is he? Are you sure he's okay?"

"Upstairs. He wanted to leave Gillham, but Kam told him he shouldn't. He told him that even though he's not a council assassin, he's with us, which means the pack and the council will protect him."

Tali swallowed. He didn't know his mate well since they

hadn't been talking, but he'd been observing Julian from afar. He knew that even though Julian was a professional assassin—and not for the same reason the assassins were—he wasn't a bad person. He had honor, and he wanted to protect people. He wanted to make sure that people who couldn't protect themselves were safe. It couldn't be easy for him to obey Kam's orders and stay in Gillham, not when he could be putting the entire pack in danger. "How did he take it?"

"Not great. He's been frowning a lot since he came back. I thought you should know."

Tali didn't ask him why. Most of the people in the warehouse didn't know he and Julian were mates, but they no doubt had noticed how they behaved with each other. "Thank you."

"It's fine. We have to look out for each other, don't we? We're a family."

Tali kissed Dasha's cheek. "Still. Thank you. I doubt Julian would have told me."

"You should talk to him."

Tali was planning on doing just that, but he didn't know when or how.

They all gathered for dinner in the dining room. Tonight, it was Rocco and Cam's turn to cook, so the food would be edible, even though Cam was still having trouble staying on his feet for long. Tali kept an eye on Julian as the evening passed, and he could tell something was wrong. Julian was never quiet. He was always laughing, talking, and making jokes. He was an upbeat kind of person, but tonight, something was *clearly* wrong.

Tali decided to keep an eye on him. He knew what was going on, and he knew how guilty Julian had to feel about putting the pack and everyone else in danger. Julian was a protector, and he cared about the assassins, even though he hadn't been with them long. This was hard for him, and he no doubt wanted to go out there and try to get rid of the people after him on his own now that he knew who they were.

It terrified Tali. He understood why Julian felt that way, but he didn't want Julian to go. He didn't want to risk him when he was just coming to terms with the fact that he wanted him in his life.

He probably should have chosen better timing.

But it was what it was, and there was nothing he could do about it. He wasn't sure he should talk to Julian, though. Julian had obviously more important things to focus on, and even though Tali had promised they'd talk, he'd done it before all of this happened.

"Stop moping," Roark said, looking at Julian.

Julian looked at him, blinking. "I'm sorry?"

Roark looked around the table. "Look, we're family, right?"

Julian hesitated. "I know you consider each other family, and I like that. I'm not part of your group, though. I'm not part of your *family*."

Roark's gaze moved to Tali, and Tali realized he was aware of the fact that they were mates. How, Tali didn't know, and he didn't care, if it meant Roark would be able to convince Julian to stay. "I don't believe that. Even if it weren't for Tali here, you've been living with us for a while. We've gotten used to having you with us, and we don't want you to leave."

Julian put down his fork. He hadn't been eating a lot, and he didn't look like he was going to empty his plate. "How can you talk like that? I'm putting everyone in danger just by being here. If the Family finds out where I am, they *will* send someone to get me, and you know the pack already has enough to worry about with that guy planning on attacking them."

Roark crossed his arms over his chest. "But you heard Kam. He's the alpha, and he's decided that he wants you to stay."

"It doesn't mean it's the right thing to do. His pack will be in danger if the Family finds out where I am, and they always do."

"They didn't find you at the warehouse."

"That's because of how secure it is—was. Only a handful of people know about it, excluding you guys, so it wouldn't have been easy for them to find me there. The pack is different, though, and with everything going on, there are a lot of people moving around. Anyone could notice me and tell someone else, or the Family directly. I can't risk it."

Roark looked around the table. "I know not all of us are here, but I think I speak for everyone when I say that we don't want you to go. We can help you. We're not going on missions right now since we don't have a home base, so we can deal with the Family."

Julian leaned back, clearly surprised. "I don't know why you think you can. The Family is big, and they're all cruel assholes. You shouldn't be involved in this. You have nothing to do with it. It's my problem to solve."

"It *was* your problem to solve. You're not alone anymore."

Julian pressed his lips together. "You're right. I'm not, and I don't know if that's a good thing."

He was planning something. That much was obvious to Tali, and he knew he would have to make sure nothing happened. Julian was a good person, but he was also stubborn, and his protective streak was a mile wide. If he thought he was protecting people, he might do something stupid, and Tali couldn't allow anything to happen to his mate.

Julian looked around the bedroom. He hadn't had much to pack to begin with, and he made sure to take only the indispensable. He was on the run, not going on vacation. He only needed a change of clothes, his weapons, and some money.

He was going to miss this place. He was going to miss the assassins even more, but he tried not to think about that. He knew they wanted to help him, and he was touched. It was one of the reasons he couldn't stay. He couldn't put them at risk, not when they'd already done so much for him.

When he'd first contacted them by sneaking into the warehouse, he hadn't thought they would help him. He'd been on the run, tired, hungry, and hyper-vigilant. He'd needed a break, and they'd given that to him. To his surprise, they'd also given him a safe place to stay, and he'd agreed because he'd known the warehouse couldn't be easily found. The only reason he had was that he'd been following Roark for years.

It was over, though. The warehouse had been attacked, and it was out of commission. It made Julian vulnerable and more easily found, so he had to go, no matter what Roark said.

The council assassins were more than able to protect themselves, but they weren't the only ones at risk here. Julian couldn't stop thinking about Tali and what might happen to him if the Family got their hands on him. If they found out he was Julian's mate, they wouldn't hesitate to use him to get to Julian, and Julian couldn't allow that to happen.

He couldn't allow anyone to be in danger because of him.

So he was leaving. He knew Roark would be pissed when he found him gone tomorrow morning, but Julian would be far away by then, and the pack and the assassins would be safe. Julian would miss being part of this, and he would miss Tali, but it was for the best.

He waited until he heard everyone going to bed. People talked outside his bedroom, saying good night to each other, closing their doors. Once they were all in their bedrooms, he waited some more. By the time it was one AM, he was tired but more than ever convinced that he needed to do this.

He grabbed his backpack, pulled it onto his shoulder, and

silently opened the door. He'd written a note so Roark and the others would know what had happened and why he'd left, and he snatched it from the dresser. He'd put it on the kitchen table for tomorrow morning.

He walked down the stairs, careful not to make them creak. There was no sound in the house, so everyone was no doubt sleeping. Leaving hurt, and even though he knew this was the best thing he could do, it didn't help that he wanted to stay anyway.

The assassins felt like a second family. Julian had his parents and his siblings, and they loved him. He loved them, too. They would help him in a second if he told them what was going on, but he didn't want to involve them. He cared too much about them, and even though being professional killers was a family business, they weren't as well equipped as the council assassins were.

He hadn't cared about the assassins when he'd first reached out, and he hadn't been sure they would help after what he'd done to them. But now he cared about them too, which made everything more complicated. It was only a matter of time before the Family found him. That was why he had to leave—so they wouldn't hurt the people he cared for. He didn't know where he would go, but this was the only thing he could do.

He got to the entrance. He paused when he reached the front door, looking around one last time. He peered up the stairs, almost expecting someone to be there. He *wanted* someone to wake up and to notice he was gone. He wanted someone to tell him that he was a dumbass—that he had to stay where he was. He wanted to belong here with the assassins, just like he belonged with his parents.

He had to get himself out of trouble first, though. Maybe once this was over and he'd gotten rid of the Family, he could come back.

He softly snorted to himself, careful not to make too much noise. He couldn't get rid of the Family. There were too many of them. Maybe, if he was lucky, he could get rid of the men after him. He didn't know for sure who was in charge of the Family now that he'd killed its head, but he had no doubt that man was the person giving the orders, so it had to be Luciano. Julian could either try to convince him to take a step back — although he doubted that would be possible — or kill him.

It was what he did. Julian was a professional killer, and even though no one had hired him for the job, it wouldn't stop him. He needed to be safe, and he needed to make sure the Family wouldn't come after the assassins or anyone else helping him.

He reached for the door handle.

The light in the entrance turned on.

Julian blinked, the sudden light blinding him. He had no idea what was going on, but he was ready to fight if he needed to.

"What do you think you're doing?" Tali asked.

Julian's heart skipped a beat. "Tali?"

Tali was standing in front of him with his arms crossed over his chest. He looked angry, and Julian knew he'd been caught. Still, he had to try to convince Tali that he had to go.

"You know what I'm doing," he said.

Tali's eyes narrowed even more. Julian couldn't remember seeing him so angry, and he didn't like it, especially not when it was aimed at him.

"You're sneaking out. You're running away," Tali accused.

"I'm not running away. I'm trying to keep you and everyone else safe."

"That's what I was saying. You're running. Roark and everyone else told you that you needed to stay. We told you we're family and that we would take care of you and protect you, yet you didn't listen. You don't want to be here with us."

Julian reached for Tali, but he didn't touch him, even though there was nothing he wanted more. "I'm trying to protect you. Can't you see that?"

Tali shook his head. "I don't believe it. You promised me you weren't going anywhere. You said you were here to stay. That's why I agreed to talk to you."

"And I would have stayed if I hadn't found out who was after me. They're dangerous, Tali. I can't allow them to hurt you. I wouldn't be able to live with myself if they did."

"So you're going to protect me by running."

"Yes." Julian was relieved Tali understood.

Then he realized that Tali was still angry.

Tali took a step forward. "I know I'm not a council assassin, but I *can* defend myself. I've been trained," Tali spat out.

"I have no doubt you can defend yourself. But the Family isn't made of normal criminals. They're dangerous. Hell, they manage to find me every time I move, and I'm not even sure how."

Tali frowned. "Is it dangerous for you to go? Will they find you eventually?"

"Probably, which is why I have to go. I can't lead them to the pack."

"So it's better to be on your own when you know they're probably going to kill you?" Tali's voice rose, and Julian prayed no one would wake up.

"Don't you see? Even if they catch me, they'll only hurt *me*. You guys will be safe. Isn't that what you want?"

"It's not," Tali paused. "I want you to be safe, too. I want you to stay with me like you promised. We're mates, Julian. How can you make this kind of decision without talking to me?"

"*You* didn't want to talk to me," Julian murmured.

"Well, I changed my mind. Talk, now. I'm listening."

Tali could see Julian was unhappy and that he wanted to go, but there was no way he would allow his mate out of the door. He stared at Julian, waiting for him to talk.

Julian huffed in frustration. "You already know what's going on. Why are you doing this, Tali? I know you want me to stay, but you have to see this is safer for everyone."

Tali shook his head. "You don't have any more reasons than you had at dinner. You just want to be a lone wolf and do everything on your own, just like you've always done. That's over, though. You have us now. You have a family."

"You think I didn't have a family before? I have parents," Julian snapped.

"And what would they say if they knew what you're doing?" Tali asked. He was kind of surprised at hearing that Julian had a family, although he wasn't sure why. He and Jolyn were orphans, but not everyone was. Most of the council assassins didn't have their family anymore, but some did, and it made Tali happy for them.

"I can't put anyone in danger, you or them. Please, Tali. Let me go."

Instead of moving from his spot by the door, Tali took his phone out of his pocket. He quickly texted Roark, knowing it wouldn't take long for him to come downstairs.

Tali had known Julian was up to something, and he'd mentioned it to Roark after dinner. He and Roark had talked for a bit, and they'd agreed that Julian would try to sneak out. They'd also agreed that Tali would be the one meeting him downstairs rather than Roark. Tali had wanted to try to convince Julian to stay on his own, but it clearly wasn't working.

"What are you doing?" Julian asked. "Who are you texting?"

"Roark. He knows about this. He'll be downstairs soon."

Julian raked a hand through his hair. "Why are you doing

this? Can't you see that this is safer for everyone?"

"Except for you, and you can stop repeating yourself. I know you think this is the best thing you can do, and that's bullshit."

"My safety doesn't matter. I'm trying to keep you and the assassins safe."

"Why did you come to us in the first place, then?"

"Because it was okay in the warehouse. It was hidden, and no one knew about it. It was also shielded against most supernatural creatures, so there would be no way for the Family to find me there, although I wasn't planning on staying long. But now things are different. We're in the middle of the Gillham pack, and there's no way the Family won't find me. We don't have the security of the warehouse anymore, and that means I have to go. I'm sorry to leave you behind, but I promise you I'll be back if I can."

Tali didn't think Julian was lying. But what if the Family, as he called them, caught him? Tali wouldn't find out, and Julian would never come back. Tali would be left with a sense of unknown grief, and he couldn't deal with that, not after losing everything else. He finally had a family back. He had a home, people he loved. He wanted his mate, too, even if that made him selfish.

They heard a door close upstairs, and they both turned toward the stairs. Roark was wearing pajama pants and a t-shirt, but he didn't look sleepy. If anything, he looked angry, and Tali was grateful. Maybe Julian would listen to him, even though he hadn't listened to his mate.

"So Tali was right," Roark said as he reached the entrance.

Julian shook his head. "You don't understand."

"I understand very well."

"I have to stay away from everyone else."

"The pack is safe, or as safe as it can be. We'll make sure nothing happens to you," Roark tried.

Tali could see it didn't convince Julian. He didn't know if anything could. It was a problem, and a problem he didn't know how to solve.

Julian wanted to be isolated. The warehouse had been good for that because only a few people knew about it, but it was also shielded. Nix couldn't shimmer inside, apart for the ones who lived there. They had a special code they entered in their phones that made the shields lower when they shimmered. Julian had been as safe as possible when he'd been in the warehouse, but now, he wasn't.

Tali understood why Julian was freaking out, but he didn't think going off on his own was the best idea. People were usually stronger together, especially when they loved each other. He and Roark had to convince Julian of that, but he didn't know how.

"I can't allow you to go out on your own," Roark said.

"I'm not one of your assassins. You can't order me around." Julian looked angry.

It was partly Tali's fault. He had to find a solution.

"Don't you see? Even though you're trying to do the right thing, it's going to be the wrong thing, at least for you. Yes, you might be able to keep the rest of us safe, but what's going to happen to you? You said yourself that the Family manages to find you every time you move. The only place in which you were safe was the warehouse."

"So I'll continue moving. Even if they get to me, if I'm always on the move, they can't reach me."

"They could. And what's going to happen if they do? What if they catch you?"

Julian's shoulders slumped. "Then I guess they'll kill me. Maybe it's what I deserve."

Those words alarmed Tali, and he reached for Julian. They'd never touched, had never held hands, but he couldn't stay back when his mate was saying that maybe he deserved to die. He took one of Julian's hands and squeezed it. Julian's eyes flew wide in shock, but Tali ignored it. "You do *not* deserve to die. You deserve to live, and to give me a chance."

"I want to. I can't risk your life, though," Julian said.

It was incredibly frustrating. Tali wanted to do something, but what? Julian was stubborn, maybe the most stubborn man Tali had ever met, and breaking through was going to be hard, if not impossible.

"We can move you somewhere else," Roark tried. "If that's what you really want, we can make sure you're in a safe place. I don't like it, but at least we'll know where you are."

"My tribe," Tali said before he could think better of it. When he did, though, he could see it was the perfect solution.

Both Roark and Julian blinked at him. "Your tribe?"

"Yes. Well, the tribe that helped Jolyn and me out of the lab. We can go there."

"What are you talking about?" Julian asked.

Tali swallowed. "You know Jolyn and I were in a lab, right? Along with Madison?"

Julian nodded. "I've heard the story, yes."

"Well, we didn't escape on our own. There's a tribe that made it a mission to save shifters and other creatures from the labs. Well, they did in the past. Things have changed, so they probably don't anymore. Anyway, when they saved us, they allowed us to stay with them. Since Jolyn and I didn't have a tribe anymore, we decided to make that place our own, at least until we were contacted to become part of the council assassins' organization. Will you be safe there?"

"But I'll be putting other people in danger."

"Maybe, but they're used to it. They raided labs, Julian. I'll contact them to make sure it's okay with them, but I think they will. You'll be isolated, and outside the tribe, there aren't a lot of people who know about the place."

"The Family might still find me there."

"They might, but I know the tribe has blockers. It's not as secure as the warehouse, but it's even more isolated." Tali prayed he was doing the right thing, and more importantly, that Julian would agree. It was the best and only idea Tali had.

He knew the tribe could keep Julian safe, and he would do his part, too. Now, Julian had to take the next step, and Tali hoped it would be the right one.

CHAPTER THREE

Julian wasn't sure that agreeing to go with Tali to stay with his tribe was the best idea he'd ever had. He hadn't been able to say no, though, not when Tali had been staring at him with pain in his eyes and Roark had been waiting for him to do just that.

He didn't like the thought of putting someone else in danger, and that was exactly what he would be doing by going there. Sure, he wouldn't be putting the council assassins in danger anymore, but it didn't mean Tali's tribe deserved to take their place. Julian had half a mind to sneak out and run away before he and Tali had to leave, but he doubted he would succeed. Now that Roark knew what he was planning, he no doubt would keep an eye on him.

It was both frustrating and nice at the same time. Julian wasn't used to having to tell anyone what he was doing, but he also didn't mind it, or at least he wouldn't have minded in any other situation. He wanted to have friends, his own family, and he felt he could have that with the assassins. On the other hand, he didn't like having to obey Roark's orders, especially when he wasn't an assassin. But there was no way out of it. Julian had come here because he knew the assassins could help him, and they were trying to, so he couldn't push them away.

He couldn't push his *mate* away.

He'd tried to. He'd thought he could sneak out before anyone noticed, and he'd left a note for Roark and Tali. He should have realized people knew him well enough to understand what he was planning. Tali had been the one to notice it, and he'd decided to do something about it. That was how Julian had been caught, and now, he wondered if his mate had been watching him.

He had been watching *Tali*, after all.

Julian left his bedroom after a night of little sleep. He wasn't looking forward to leaving Gillham and the few assassins living here for now. He would miss them, even though he would never admit that to their face, especially not when it came to Roark. He also wasn't looking forward to living with the tribe, mostly because he knew that most Nix tribes lived in the middle of the forest with no running water or electricity, and because he didn't want to put them in danger. He'd agreed to go, though, and there was no coming back from it. He was pretty sure both Tali and Roark would hunt his ass down and drag him back if he tried to sneak away.

Julian went downstairs, carrying his backpack like he had last night. This time was very different, though. It wasn't dark outside, and sunlight streamed through the windows. He could smell the scents of breakfast. His stomach rumbled, and he moved toward the kitchen, eager to have some bacon and eggs.

People were already in the kitchen, eating and talking. Tali was present, along with Roark and a few others, and Tali and Roark were talking quietly. Tali looked up when he heard Julian, though, and he smiled.

"Are you ready?" he asked as he moved closer.

Julian grimaced. "Can we eat breakfast first?"

"Of course. I'll fix you a plate."

"Can I have some bacon and eggs, please?"

Tali smiled softly. "I know what you like for breakfast, Julian. Sit down."

The others were acting as if Julian wasn't even in the room, although he did get a few smiles. He was pretty sure everyone knew he'd tried to sneak out, and he wasn't sure if they were angry at him or if it was something else. He didn't quite fit in with them yet, but he hoped that eventually, he would. He wasn't too sure about that anymore, but he supposed he would see what happened next.

A plate appeared on the table in front of him, and he turned to smile at Tali. "Thank you."

Tali nodded and sat next to him, his own plate in hand. "You're welcome. Do you want to talk about it?"

"Talk about what?" Julian asked as he speared a piece of egg with this fork.

"About the fact that you're freaking out about going to the tribe. You're scared to put them in danger, aren't you?"

Julian sighed. "Of course I am. Anyone who's close to me right now is in danger, and that's the last thing I want to take to the tribe."

"You had no problem coming to us in the beginning."

"Because I knew where you lived. I'd been watching the warehouse, and I knew how secure it was. The only reason I managed to sneak in was that I was lucky, and I happened to be there when the power went out. I wouldn't have been able to otherwise."

"Why did you sneak in in the first place? I mean, if you wanted help, you could have just contacted us. What were you planning on doing on your own?"

Julian could feel his mate's gaze on him, but he focused on his plate. "Honestly, I'm not sure. I guess I was trying to hide, and it was too good a chance to waste it. I was planning on maybe hiding under furniture or something and waiting for the evening to come. Then, during the night, I could've shifted and eaten and made sure Roark found me sitting at the dining table in the morning." Julian chuckled. "I can imagine how shocked he would have been."

"But instead, we found you," Roark said, his voice strong.

Julian grinned at him and shrugged. "I can't say it ended badly, though." He sobered up. "But I truly don't want anyone to get hurt because of me."

Tali pushed his eggs around his plate, not looking at Julian. "I understand why you don't want that to happen. But the tribe is used to this kind of thing. They're ready for it. They're even ready for an attack, if that's what you're thinking about."

"How can they be? No one can always be ready for an attack."

"I told you what they did. They used to rescue people in the labs and fought the company that held them there. And now, since the labs are back, they're gearing up for another fight. They want to start saving people from the labs again, and they're more than happy to have you there with them."

Julian wasn't convinced, but there was nothing he could do. He hoped Tali was right about tribe security. He hadn't explained what the village was like in detail, but he'd promised the tribe had a security system in place. Besides, it was isolated, and barely anyone knew it was there. That was for a good reason, of course, since the tribe rescued people from the labs, and Julian hoped it was in the middle of nowhere. If the Family didn't know he was there, it would give him a few days at the very least. They didn't know about Tali, and they wouldn't look for Julian at the village. Hopefully, that wouldn't change anytime soon, but Julian was ready to leave if that was the case. He didn't know how he would manage, since apparently the only way to get to and out of the village was by shimmering, but if it came to it, he'd find a way.

He might be agreeing to do this, but the first thing he had in mind was Tali's safety. His came second, and he would make sure that Tali was safe and healthy, even if it was to his detriment. If it came to it, he would surrender himself to the Family. If that was the only way to make sure Tali was okay, Julian wouldn't even hesitate.

It didn't make sense, but then, feelings rarely did.

Julian sneaked a peek at Tali, but Tali was talking with his brother, who was sitting on his other side, and he didn't look back at Julian.

Julian didn't want to lose this. He didn't want to lose Tali, the assassins, the possibility of having a family of his own. If he had to, he would leave everything behind, though. He was ready to do just about anything to keep his mate safe.

"I want you to be bonded the next time we see each other," Jolyn said.

Tali rolled his eyes. "That's not going to happen."

"You can't know that. You're going to be stuck in the village with Julian for who knows how long. It's the best opportunity you'll have to get to know him, make him fall in love with you, and bond with you."

Tali laughed. "You sound like you want me to force him or something."

"Of course not. But it's obvious both of you are interested in the other, and I think this is the best chance you'll have to spend some time alone. As soon as the warehouse is ready, we'll be moving in, and then life as we know it will start again. You'll both be busy, and you won't have as much time with Julian as you do now. Take advantage of it, Tali."

Tali shook his head. He wouldn't be bonding with Julian. Julian barely looked at him, and he'd had to threaten him to get him to go to the tribe with him. He was pretty sure that if Julian had a chance, he would sneak out and leave, and Tali would be left alone with his feelings.

No. He had to focus on keeping Julian safe. That was the best thing he could do, and whatever he felt wasn't going to stop him. He wasn't an assassin, and he wasn't a fighter, but that didn't mean he couldn't protect Julian, especially from himself.

He understood Julian better now. Julian might be a professional killer, but from what Tali knew about him, he only took jobs that meant he would be killing people who deserved to be killed. He was a bit like the assassins that way. He might not work for the council, but their jobs were similar, which explained why both he and Roark had been sent to kill the same man.

Julian was a protector. Tali was pretty sure he didn't think of himself that way, but there was no denying it. His first instinct was always to protect people, which was why he'd tried to sneak out. He would no doubt do the same thing once they got to the village, and Tali would have to be careful. He had to keep an eye on Julian and make sure he didn't do something stupid like sneaking away and find himself on his own. He might not be putting anyone in danger if he was alone, but he hadn't realized that he was putting *himself* in danger that way.

The tribe knew everything that was happening, and they'd agreed to welcome Julian anyway. Julian wouldn't understand, but Tali did. He'd lived with the tribe for a while after they'd rescued him and his brother, and they were good people. They truly believed in what they did, which was why the members were a hodgepodge of Nix, but also shifters and even a few humans. It was a made-up tribe, very much like the council assassins were a made-up family, and it was lovely. Tali had always felt at home there.

"Ready?" Roark asked as he walked into the entrance.

Tali hugged his brother one last time, then stepped closer to Julian. "As ready as we can be," he said.

Roark smiled at him. They'd talked about what would happen this morning, and they had a plan. Tali was supposed to keep Julian at the village as long as possible and to make sure he didn't disappear during the night. In the meantime, Roark and a few other assassins would come up with a plan to deal with the Family. Julian wouldn't be happy to find out about it, but it was the safest option for everyone, and hopefully, he'd see that once Roark explained what he'd come up with.

Julian was used to being on his own, which made sense since he was a professional killer, but now that he was close to the assassins, he had to learn to work with people. It would no doubt take time, but this was the first step, even though he didn't know it.

"Stay safe, both of you," Roark said. He turned his attention to Julian. "And you, don't run away like an idiot. I know you don't want to put people in danger, but this tribe is used to it. They can help you, even though you don't think so. You don't have to think that everyone is weak and can't deal with the situation."

Julian spluttered. "That's not what I think. I know the assassins are strong, but that doesn't mean I was happy to bring my problems to you. The same goes for the tribe."

Roark arched a brow. "Why did you come to us if you didn't want to dump your problems on us?"

Julian shook his head. "I didn't have other options. It was either that or get killed. I have regrets, to be honest. I pulled you and your people into the middle of danger, and I don't like it. I like even less doing it to this tribe."

Tali huffed, but he realized that no amount of telling Julian he was wrong would help. Maybe things would be different if he saw it with his own two eyes, and Tali was eager to shimmer them to the tribe.

Roark shook his head, his expression halfway between frustration and amusement. "You're one of the most stubborn people I've ever met. I know that nothing I can say will make you change your mind about putting people in danger, so I won't try again. But you know you're in danger, Julian. You know that if you're not careful, the Family *will* kill you. You don't want that to happen, and neither do I or anyone else here. Be careful. Don't do anything on impulse. If you need help, any kind of help, contact me. You have my phone number and Win's."

Julian nodded reluctantly, and Tali looked at Roark. They had their job cut out for them, but that wouldn't stop Julian from doing it.

His first job would be to keep Julian safe. If he managed that, he could move on to their personal relationship. They hadn't talked about it yet, but hopefully, now that they would have time, they would.

They left the house, and Tali didn't look back. He wasn't leaving forever, and once he was back, his brother would be right here where he'd left him. Jolyn would be safe with the other assassins in the Gillham pack territory. It was just about the safest place he could be right now.

"Ready?" Tali asked as he and Julian reached one of the spots in which Nix could shimmer in and out of pack territory. It had been opened especially for them this morning, since usually, it was closed off now that the pack had been threatened, but Kameron knew what was happening, and he wanted to help. Tali was relieved they didn't have to walk out of pack territory, mostly because he couldn't be sure whether or not the Family knew Julian was here.

"We should talk," Julian said.

Tali almost snorted. Of course he wanted to talk now. "Do you really think this is the right time?"

"Probably not. But I'm about to walk into a place I don't know, and I have doubts. You know that. You're aware of the fact that I still think that leaving would be best for everyone."

"I don't see what that has to do with talking now. I'm sure it can wait at least ten minutes until we get to the village."

"I want to know what's going on between us before we get there. I want to know whether or not you'll be my ally. More importantly, I want to be sure things won't be awkward between us if we're forced to live together for who knows how long."

Tali was mildly offended that Julian seemed to think he wouldn't be his ally. "Fine. We can talk. What do you want to know?"

Julian stared at him for a moment. "You know what I want to know. We were supposed to talk, and now, we have time. We're alone, and no one will listen to us. Tell me, Tali. What do you want from me?"

Tali sucked in a breath. He hadn't expected the question, and he wasn't quite sure how to answer it.

Julian could agree this probably wasn't the best moment or place to ask Tali about his feelings, but he needed to know. He needed to know before they went to the village, where Tali would be the only person Julian knew.

Julian usually had an easy time making friends, but he wasn't going to the tribe to make friends. He didn't want to get to know the people he was putting in danger, especially when he felt so guilty about it. He realized he wouldn't be able to isolate himself. Since the tribe was welcoming him, he had every intention of helping where he could. He wouldn't be a kept man, but he didn't know how much he would be able to do. He didn't know how the tribe worked or what they would need from him.

But he wanted to have at least one person on his side, and that person was Tali.

Julian had wanted that since the beginning, when he'd realized Tali was his mate. He wanted to ask why Tali hadn't said anything when he'd found out, but so far, he hadn't. He didn't want to freak Tali out, but since they were going to spend a lot of time together, it was better to be honest.

Besides, he wanted to take a chance on them. He had to see if they could be a couple and work as one. There was no way to know what his life would be like tomorrow, or the day after that, or next week, but if he could have Tali by his side, maybe it wouldn't be all bad. He would have to be careful and shield Tali from the Family, but he thought he could, especially since Tali was so important to the assassins. They were Tali's family, and they would kick Julian's ass if he didn't make sure he was safe.

"What do you want to know?" Tali asked.

"Well, we haven't talked about this at all. We both know we're mates, but that's it. I want to know what you want from me, Tali. I want to know what you expect. What you dream of."

"Those are a lot of questions."

"You don't have to answer any of them if you're not comfortable. I just hope you'll give me a chance."

He hadn't until now, and Julian didn't understand why. He realized he didn't know much about his mate, though. Tali had been taken from his tribe and put in a lab with his twin, where they'd been tortured. They'd been rescued by their new tribe, and they'd stayed there for a bit until they'd been contacted by the council. Then they'd moved in with the council assassins, and they'd been living and working there since then.

That was it. Julian didn't know anything else about his mate's history. He *did* know that Tali was sweet, gentle, and quiet. He knew that he was caring, and that he had his favorites when it came to the assassins. He would never say it out loud, but Julian had eyes, and he could see it.

So maybe he did know a bit about Tali, but it wasn't enough. He needed more.

"You want to know why I didn't talk to you right away when I realized we were mates," Tali said as he looked away.

"I do. I've been thinking about that since I realized you didn't. I don't understand. I don't know if it's because you don't like me, or because you didn't want anything to do with me, or something else. I'm a bit lost, and while I don't want to push you, I'd like some answers."

Tali sighed. "It had nothing to do with you, not the way you think. Things have been hectic, and when I first saw you, it wasn't the best time to tell you. We weren't even in the warehouse, and you needed protection."

Julian remembered. He'd seen Tali at the pool when the assassins had temporarily left the warehouse because the AC wasn't working during a heatwave. They'd been taken in by one of the mates' mothers, who had a big house that included a pool. Tali had been gorgeous wearing only swimming trunks, and Julian had found himself attracted to him right away, even though he hadn't known they were mates yet.

"What about after we went back to the warehouse? Why didn't you tell me then?" he asked.

Tali sighed. "I wanted to. Trust me. I didn't know if I should, though."

"Why not?"

"Because I thought you were going to leave eventually. You made sure to tell Roark and Win that you wanted time to breathe. You told them that as soon as you could, you were going to go, so I knew that I had to choose between you and the assassins."

That made sense, no matter how little Julian liked it. "And you chose the assassins."

"I can't *not* choose them. They're my family, Julian. The only family I have."

"Didn't you say that you also had the tribe? This new tribe, I mean."

"I do have them. Jolyn and I stayed with them for a bit, and they were welcoming. We visit them, and we do consider

Alvar and Emelie our surrogate parents, but it's not the same. They're like extended family, people you call every so often for their birthdays and Christmas. But the assassins, well, I live with them. I talk to them every day, and if something happens, they're the first people I think to ask for help. I hope you understand, but you don't have to accept this. I'll understand if you can't."

Julian did understand, and he didn't have anything to accept. This was Tali, and if he wanted his mate, he would have to accept him as he was, including how close he was to the assassins. "What about now? Do you still think I'm going to leave?"

Tali shrugged and looked away again. "I don't know. I know you said you wanted to, but everything is so complicated, and I don't expect you to make decisions immediately. It wouldn't be fair, not in this situation."

Julian didn't like that Tali seemed to think he wasn't allowed to demand things from him. They were mates, and it meant something to him — that he wanted to be with Tali — and he would do everything he could to make that happen.

But he had to get rid of the Family first, and he didn't know if that was possible.

He sighed. "I do want to be with you, and I'm not planning on leaving, not if I can help it."

Tali looked at him, a smile forming on his face.

Julian hated to destroy that hope, but he had to. "I can't make promises," he continued. "I might not want to go, but you know the situation. You know the Family is after me, and that they're dangerous. I might want to be with you, but I want to keep you safe even more."

Tali's smile fell, then Julian could see a hint of stubbornness in his gaze. "I understand. It doesn't mean I agree with what you're saying, though."

"You don't have to. This is a decision I have to make."

"So you truly think you have to choose between being with me and keeping me safe?"

"I do. The Family could find out about you, and if they do, they'll try to use you against me." If that happened, Julian would go, even though it would hurt. He couldn't protect himself while leaving Tali in danger.

Tali sighed and held a hand out. "Fine. I understand where you're coming from, and I see your point of view. I can't say I like it, but I won't push. If you truly think you need to leave because it's the only way to keep me safe, then go. But you know where to find me, and I'll wait for you."

"I can't demand that you wait for me." Especially if there was a possibility that Julian would be killed.

"It's a good thing you're not asking, then. I was afraid you would leave, and I still am. I can't deny the fact that we're mates, though, and that I want you. So do what you have to do, Julian. Once you're done, I'll be home waiting for you."

Julian wanted to protest, but he could tell he wouldn't change Tali's mind. So instead, he took Tali's hand and allowed him to shimmer them to the tribe.

Tali didn't like how the conversation had gone. He wanted Julian to stay, but he could tell he wouldn't be able to force him into doing anything. So he shimmered them to the tribe.

There was a particular spot in which all the Nix who belonged to the tribe had to shimmer. Since the tribe was closed off and shielded, they couldn't shimmer directly into the village, but that was a good thing. It gave Tali the time to wrap his mind around the conversation he'd had with Julian.

He didn't like the thought of Julian leaving, even though he understood why Julian might think he had to. He wanted them to have a chance, though.

When they arrived, he didn't move. Instead, he stood there,

trying to put his thoughts into words. "If you had a choice and no one was in danger, would you want to stay?" he finally asked.

Julian's expression softened. "More than anything. But even if the family wasn't hunting me, I might not be allowed to stay. I'm not a council assassin, and I can never be one. I'm only a shifter, while the assassins are special. I don't know if I *can* stay—only Win and the council can decide that—but I don't want to leave you behind or to lose everything I gained while I was staying with you and the assassins."

Tali slowly nodded. He understood what Julian was saying, and he knew it was true. The council assassins were all special in a way, even though most of them hated that and the way they had become special. They had powers no one else had, except for Tali and his brother. They were just Nix, but they were healers, and that was what they'd been doing for years.

What would Julian's role with the assassins be, though? If he stayed with them, he couldn't truly be part of their group. He wouldn't be sent on missions by the council. Maybe he could still accept jobs on his own, but Tali didn't know how that would work. He hoped Win and Roark would want Julian to stay, and he didn't want to think about what would happen if they didn't.

But he wanted to continue living with the others at the new warehouse. He wanted Julian, for them to be close, maybe even to bond. He didn't know if that was possible, but it was what he wanted to work toward.

"Tali?" Julian asked. He sounded hesitant, as if he expected a rejection.

Tali didn't understand why. He hadn't rejected Julian before, not really. He'd just asked for time, and he'd gotten it. Now, that time was over, and they had to have this discussion. Tali felt like they were talking in circles, though. They hadn't decided anything except that Julian would leave if he thought he was putting Tali in danger, and he still didn't feel like they'd put all the cards on the table.

It looked like he would have to be the one to do that.

He let go of Julian's hand and moved in front of him. "All right. So, you're not sure you'll be able to stay. I know it doesn't entirely depend on you, and I understand. But I want you, Julian. We're mates, and I want that kind of bond and relationship with you."

"What did you have in mind?" Julian asked.

It took Tali by surprise. He'd thought Julian would agree or disagree. Either Julian would want to be with him, or he would push him away to keep him safe. Instead, Julian was taking his time to think about it, and possibly see if they could somehow fit together. "Well, eventually, I want us to bond and live together. It's what we're supposed to do."

"But not what we *have* to do. We have a choice, even though we're mates."

"Fine. It's what I *want* to do, then."

"You could change your mind. Maybe you'll hate me once you get to know me."

Tali snorted. "I doubt it. I might not talk to you often, but I've been watching you. I like what I see, and I want to discover more about you." He paused, licking his lips. "Maybe that's what we can do. We can get to know each other while we're stuck here. Let's not make any kind of promises neither of us knows if we can keep. We can just get to know each other, spend time together, and see where things go." It wasn't what Tali wanted, but if it was the only thing he could get, he would take it.

Julian stared at him for a moment. Then, he slowly nodded, and Tali knew he'd gotten what he wanted, at least in part.

"All right. Let's do that," Julian agreed.

Tali nodded and offered Julian his hand again, and this

time, Julian didn't hesitate. He took it and linked their fingers together, then, he looked around. "So, where's this village you've been talking about?"

It looked like the discussion was over, but that was fine. If they needed to, they could talk about it again. If they didn't, well, they'd made their decision for now.

Tali pulled him forward. "This way. Like I told you, the village in which the tribe lives is shielded. That was needed when they raided labs, and since they've started again, I can't imagine they'll let their guard down. It's not far, though."

"Will they be surprised to see us?"

"No. They know everything that happens around here, so they're aware we've arrived."

Julian looked impressed, and he didn't have any more questions until they reached the village.

Tali turned to look at him when they did. He knew the village wasn't like most other Nix villages, and he was curious to see Julian's reaction to it.

"This isn't what I was expecting," Julian said, his eyes wide.

"It's not what anyone expects."

The tribe had lived in a normal hut village for a long time, but that had changed even before they'd rescued Tali and his brother. The huts were still there, but they were sturdier than usual, and more importantly, the tribe used solar power for electricity. It wasn't exactly a small town, but it looked like it, and Julian seemed to be impressed.

A man was waiting for them in front of the entrance to the village. He smiled at Tali when he saw him, and Tali smiled back. He'd missed Alvar, and he was eager to talk to him again. Alvar had been one of the Nix who had been at the lab when Tali had been saved, and Tali would always associate him with that time. The fact that Alvar and his mate had taken Tali and Jolyn under their wings and considered them their sons also made Tali happy, even though he wasn't as close to Alvar as he probably should be.

"Tali. Welcome back," Alvar said as they reached him.

Tali let go of Julian's hand and moved toward Alvar to hug him. "It's good to see you again."

"It really is," Alvar agreed.

They moved back, and Tali looked at Alvar. He looked a little older than the last time Tali had seen him, but he was still a strong man, the same man he'd been when he and his mate had taken in Tali and his brother and had nursed them back to health. Tali didn't have his parents anymore, but he considered Alvar and his mate a surrogate mother and father.

"Come on," Alvar said after introducing himself to Julian. "Rikar is waiting for you. He wants to talk to you and Julian."

"Of course." Tali had been looking forward to putting his feet up for a bit and relaxing, but he knew this had to be done.

"When you're done talking to him, come straight home. We have the guest room set up for you and Julian."

"I don't want to put you out," Julian said.

"Don't worry about that. We can find you another place to stay if you're not comfortable with it, but I'd still like to keep the two of you close." His gaze moved from Tali to Julian. "I can see there's something here, and I'm eager to find out."

Tali rolled his eyes. "You've always been nosy."

"Don't talk to me like that, kid. We're happy to see you again, though. We'll be waiting for you when you're done with Rikar."

Tali hadn't been sure this was a good idea, and he still wasn't, but he was relieved he'd had it. He'd missed Alvar and Emelie, and now he would have the opportunity to spend more time with them again and to keep Julian safe at the same time.

He couldn't wait.

Chapter Four

Julian and Tali had been taking things slow. It had been a week since they'd arrived at the village, and Julian was getting a bit antsy. He felt like he wasn't doing enough, considering the tribe had welcomed him, but there truly wasn't anything he could do.

He would know — he'd asked.

He didn't like feeling like they were helping him while he wasn't giving anything in return, but he couldn't deny that was what was happening. The village and the tribe were always busy, with people walking up and down the tiny village's main path. There was always something going on. Julian couldn't help but wonder what they were preparing for since they obviously were, but Tali had mentioned they were planning to help rescue people from the labs again, so it made sense.

Julian wondered if they didn't want him to help because they didn't trust him or because he was a guest. He didn't know. He would've thought the first one, but with the way everyone had been acting toward him, he couldn't be a hundred percent sure.

He walked down the street — it wasn't exactly a street, but it was much bigger than a path — as he looked around to find Tali. He waved at a few people, and they waved back, beaming at him. It had been that way since he'd arrived, and it was slightly confusing. Julian was a people-person most days, but the tribe took it to another level.

They'd all welcomed him, but especially Tali's family.

Julian knew they weren't Tali's birth parents, but he didn't think it mattered. Alvar and Emelie had taken in Tali and his brother when they needed a home, and Julian knew that Tali considered them his parents.

The tribe was big, and the village much larger than Julian had imagined, so people weren't on top of each other. Still, sometimes, he wished he and Tali could have a bit of privacy. There was always someone watching, and even if they didn't mean to, it was getting crowded. The space was what it was, and Julian wanted more, which was why he was looking for his mate. He was planning on asking him on a date, although he wasn't quite sure what they would do since they weren't supposed to leave the village.

There wasn't much to do. Even though the village was bigger than Julian had thought, it was still small, with about twenty or twenty-five huts in which people lived. There weren't any shops or anything like that. Julian couldn't take Tali for coffee or to the movies. It was out of the question, and he was sad about it. He couldn't risk the Family finding him, though. So far, they didn't seem to know where he was, and he wanted that to continue.

He'd been impressed by the security system the village had in place. He hadn't thought it possible until he'd seen it. The village was shielded from outside Nix by strong shields. They were the best that technology had come up with in the past couple of years, and Julian wondered how the village obtained them. He wasn't about to ask, though. It wasn't his business, and he doubted he would get an answer. He'd met the tribe leader, Rikar, and while the man was nice, it was obvious that Julian wasn't part of the tribe.

That was okay. He didn't want to be part of the tribe. He wanted to be able to go home at the end of this, and he found himself surprised that meant he wanted to go back to the council assassins.

When had they become his family? He hadn't spent that much time with them, just a few months, and he had a family already—his parents and siblings.

"Julian!" someone called out. Julian turned around to see Emelie, Tali's adoptive mother, on the other side of the street. She was carrying a basket and waving at him, and Julian hurried to her side, holding his hand out to take the basket from her.

She scowled at him. "I am more than capable of carrying a basket," she said. There was no heat in her voice.

"Just because you can doesn't mean you should," Julian insisted.

She blinked. "I think I heard that in a movie once."

Julian laughed. "Maybe. How do you watch movies here?"

She rolled her eyes. "You know that even though we live in the woods, we have electricity, right?"

"I know. I just didn't see a TV in your home." That had surprised Julian, too. The village had electricity and running water, as well as heating. It was all powered by solar panels, and it was impressive. He'd explored all of that over a few days right after he'd arrived, and while it was interesting, it wasn't really his thing. Still, it was impressive that the tribe had managed to put all of that together.

"We have a computer," Emelie said as they walked toward the hut.

"I didn't think about that."

"If you don't have one with you, you can borrow ours. I don't know why you don't have one. You're so young. It seems like everyone these days has a computer and a cell phone."

Julian had had to flee when the Family came after him, so he'd left most of his things behind in safe places, but she wasn't wrong. "I need to find a phone. I should call my family." They were used to not hearing from him for long periods of time, but it was becoming too long, and his parents would freak out. His sister, on the other hand, was probably happy not to have competition on the job.

Emelie's eyes widened. "Why didn't you ask? I could have given you a phone the first day. Your poor parents."

"Don't worry about it. It's not urgent. I don't call them often anyway."

"I'll give it to you right away."

"No, don't worry. I was actually looking for Tali."

She smiled softly. "How are the two of you doing?"

Both she and her mate were aware that Julian and Tali were mates, and that they weren't bonded yet. They had eyes, and they could see how awkward and careful they were around each other. They'd had questions, though, and as far as Julian knew, Tali hadn't provided information.

"I was planning on taking him on a date," Julian explained. "Although I'm not sure where we should go."

"Well, there's a town close by. You could take a walk and have lunch."

Julian hesitated. He liked that idea, but he wasn't sure it was the best one. "There are still people after me, though."

"Well, I understand, but what if you can't stop them? Will you stop living?"

She wasn't wrong. Julian didn't like the fact that he was in hiding and been on the run for months. He wanted to live his life again. He wanted to be free to do things without looking over his shoulder. That wasn't going to happen anytime soon, but maybe he could take this opportunity. He doubted the Family would find him here, not when he'd been hiding at the warehouse for months and they didn't know about Tali.

"It's not a bad idea. Where should I take him?"

Emelie grinned. "I'll help. I know what he likes."

Julian couldn't help but smile as he listened to her. She was gentle and caring, and he was glad. In the beginning, when the Family had first started coming after him, he'd thought that eventually, they would get him. He'd been alone, or so he'd believed.

He'd been wrong.

"Are you sure there's nothing I can do?" Tali asked. He was almost begging, but he was *bored*.

He loved visiting the tribe, but he didn't usually stay more than a few days. Now he'd been here a week, and he didn't know what to do with himself.

He'd helped Emelie around the house. He'd taken walks with Julian. He'd taken walks on his own. He'd talked to people he'd missed while he was away. All of that had taken only a few days, though, and he was ready to climb the walls, which was why he'd come to see Anja, the tribe healer.

She looked at him, crossing her arms over her chest. "I told you there's nothing you can do to help me."

"But I'm good at healing. I learned with the best."

"That's because you learned with *me*. I know you're good, Tali. I just don't have anyone for you to heal." She gestured around the empty hut. "You can see that for yourself."

Tali shoulders slumped. "I had to try."

"I understand. The situation isn't easy for you, but you should focus on your mate. The two of you have the opportunity to spend time together. Do that instead of annoying me."

Tali cocked his head. "How do you know he's my mate?"

"Is the sky blue? Everyone knows you're mates. It's obvious in the way you look at each other, and besides, Emelie told me."

Tali barked out a laugh. "I'm not surprised." He looked around once again, but Anja wasn't lying. There truly wasn't anything to do for one healer, let alone two. "You'll let me know if there's anything I can do to help, though?"

"I will. Stop obsessing. Take time off. I doubt you have a lot of that while you're working."

Tali had never told anyone he and Jolyn worked with the council assassins, but sometimes, a few of them had come with him and his brother, so he suspected the tribe knew. Even if they didn't recognize the assassins and didn't know much about them, they had eyes, and they'd been dealing with secrets for a long time, way before they'd rescued Tali. They didn't seem to have a problem with it, which was good. Tali didn't want to have to choose between the tribe and the assassins.

He left the hut, wondering what was next for him. He couldn't work, but he was getting bored, and he needed to do something before he went bananas.

"Tali!"

Tali jumped and looked around.

Julian was striding toward him, a smile on his face.

Tali's stomach fluttered, and he smiled even though he didn't mean to. This was what he was reduced to now — smiling every time he saw Julian.

He didn't mind. He liked Julian, and he hoped that eventually, the two of them would get to the point of having a relationship and maybe being in love.

"Julian. What are you doing here?"

"Emelie told me where to find you. She said you were bored and that you were probably going to bug the healer."

Tali scowled. "I didn't bug her. I just asked her if she needed help."

"And did she?"

"No. It has nothing to do with me, though. I asked, and she refused. That's it."

Julian was still smiling, and amusement shone in his eyes. "All right. Well, if you don't have anything else to do, let's go on a date."

Tali's brain shuttered to a stop. "A date?"

"You know, it's when two people like each other and want to see if they can be in a relationship."

Tali reached out and slapped Julian's shoulder. "I know what a date is. It's just that you've never asked me on a date, and since we're stuck here, I'm not sure what we can actually do." But Tali liked the idea. He actually *loved* it.

He'd wanted to get closer to Julian since the first day when Julian hadn't even known they were mates. He'd kept his distance, and he didn't regret it, but now, Julian knew they were mates, and Tali wanted more. The fact that they were spending a lot of time together without everyone else around was helping. Tali was falling in love with Julian, even though they weren't even together yet. He didn't know what would happen next, or in a more distant future. He just had to have faith that it would be good.

"What do you think? Emelie suggested we go into town. Maybe an hour or two, so it won't cause a problem with the Family, and we can distract ourselves a bit. I love the tribe and the village, but I'm starting to get cabin fever," Julian said.

"You're not the only one. Are you sure it's safe, though?" Because Tali would never forgive himself if something happened because Julian had wanted to take him out on a date.

Julian held a hand out. "I'm sure. Let's go."

"Now?"

"When did you want to go? Or did you have something to do?"

"I don't." And he wouldn't have Julian ask twice. He couldn't wait to get out of here, either.

Tali linked his fingers with Julian's, and together, they headed toward the entrance to the village. The guards there knew them and nodded but didn't try to stop them. That wasn't what they were there for.

Julian and Tali left the village and headed toward the spot from which they would shimmer. "What did you have in mind?" Tali asked.

"Well, I'm not really a dinner and movie kind of guy, but if that's what you want to do, we can."

"That would have to wait until later, since it's only lunchtime. How about lunch? We can take a walk while we eat, and you can see the town. It's not big, but it's home." Not as much as the village, but going there felt natural to Tali.

Julian beamed. "That sounds perfect."

So that was what they did. Tali shimmered them to town, and even though it was smaller than Gillham, it was quaint and cute. He took Julian to his favorite sandwich shop, and they grabbed something to eat before heading out again. They walked down the sidewalk, slowly eating as they talked.

"Damn, it feels good," Julian said before taking a bite out of his sandwich.

"It's been weighing on you, hasn't it?" Tali asked.

Julian chewed and swallowed before asking, "What has been?"

"Being stuck in the village."

"It has. I'm grateful to the tribe for welcoming me, and I know it's necessary, but I'm not used to being stuck in a place for so long."

"It must have been even worse with the assassins. I mean, there, you couldn't leave the warehouse. The village is a bit bigger."

"It was, but it also wasn't. I know it doesn't make sense. I like the tribe, and I like the people who live here, but they're not my family."

Tali blinked. "The assassins are, though?"

"Kind of." Julian shrugged and took another bite of his sandwich. "Maybe it's because I'd been watching you guys for a while before sneaking in. I know it makes it sound creepy, but I needed to know about you. Besides, I've known about the assassins for a while. I was in competition with them, and they took out a few of my targets, although the one Roark killed was the worst of them. But I think it's more than that. Since I've been living with you, I realized that I'm similar to most of the assassins, and it made me feel a kinship toward them, you know?"

Tali nodded. "Will you officially become a council assassin, then?" It sounded like he wanted to and like he belonged with them, and Tali couldn't say he'd be sorry to have Julian close to him.

Julian grimaced and shook his head. "I don't know. It's not a decision I can make. I'm not special like the assassins are. I'm just a normal shifter, and I don't know why the council would want me with them, especially with the trouble following me."

"The fact that you don't have any kind of power doesn't mean you can't be a council assassin. It hasn't been done before, but it's not a hard rule." Tali doubted it would be a problem, but Julian was right. It was something he would have to discuss with Win, and only the council could make that decision. "Do you *want* to be one?"

Julian looked Tali straight in the eyes. "More than anything. Well, there *is* one thing I want more than becoming a council assassin, but having a relationship with you is going to take more time."

It felt good to walk while talking with Tali. Julian couldn't remember the last time he'd done something like this. Even before the Family had decided to come after him, he didn't have a normal life. Hell, he'd *never* had a normal life.

Both his parents had been professional killers. His mom had stopped when she'd had children, but his father hadn't.

It had made for a weird family life, and both Julian and his sister had followed in their parents' footsteps. The only one who hadn't was Sam, Julian's brother, and he was kind of the black sheep of the family in that regard. Everyone loved him, and he loved them, too, but he was clearly uncomfortable with what they did.

But being professional killers meant they always had to be careful. Julian had never had many friends, and he certainly never had anyone he could walk down the sidewalk with. It felt good.

He couldn't wait to see what life with Tali would be like. He knew that once the new warehouse was ready for the assassins, they would all move there, and their life would change again. He knew that most of the assassins left the warehouse often, even when they weren't on a mission. The mated ones especially went on dates on the weekends away from the chaos of the warehouse.

Julian wanted that, too. He wanted to start the life he'd always wanted with the council assassins and his mate. It was incredible to him that it might be in reach, and that eventually, he might be able to have it.

He liked Tali, and he hoped this was the beginning of something good. He didn't know whether or not he would ever be allowed to become a council assassin, but he would ask. That was the only way he'd find out. He'd have to talk to Win and see if the man could look into it, and Julian was ready to do just that as soon as he got back with the assassins. He knew it wouldn't be easy, not with the council only hiring shifters with a special power to be their assassins. But even though Julian was a plain shifter, he had experience, and he knew he could do it.

Well, he hoped so.

He'd been watching the assassins, and while their job was made easier by what they could do, it was what Julian was used to. Julian might take longer to do things, and it might not be as easy, but it didn't mean he couldn't do it.

"I missed going out," Tali said. He tilted his face up so he could look at the sky. "I love the village and the tribe, but sometimes, it's restrictive to be there, you know?"

"You don't leave the warehouse much even when you're with the assassins, do you?"

Tali shrugged. "I don't have to. I mean, don't get me wrong, I love this, but I'm also just as happy staying at home. The tribe isn't my home anymore, though, so it makes it a bit weird. I don't know. The fact that I'm a healer for the council assassins is kind of an open secret here. I know that most of them don't understand what I do for a living. Alvar and Emelie don't care, but the tribe is all about saving people, and a few of them have made it clear that they don't want anything to do with me because of that."

"I'm sorry."

"Don't be. You have nothing to do with it. Honestly, I'm happy with the assassins. I promise. I wouldn't stay with them if I wasn't. It's a bit like having two families that are pulling you apart. There's the tribe on one side and the assassins on the other. The tribe saved me and was my home when I need them, but I have a real family now."

"It's not easy." But Julian understood the feeling of being pulled in different directions.

Tali smiled. "Is anything ever easy? Even our relationship isn't easy. We're still finding our way around each other, and I kind of wish we'd done that earlier."

"And who's fault is it that we didn't?" Julian teased. He made sure that Tali heard from his voice that he wasn't being harsh with him. He might not like that Tali didn't tell him they were mates right away, but he understood why he hadn't. Besides, he couldn't change the past.

Tali shrugged. "I freaked out. I thought you were going to

leave, and that it would be better if you didn't know we were mates."

"But now, you know I'm not going anywhere."

"I do, and I'm happy about it."

They looked at each other as they walked, which was the only reason Julian didn't notice the man who reached them. He grabbed Tali's arm and pulled him into an alley, and Julian froze for just a few seconds.

Then he followed them.

Tali might not be a council assassin, but it was obvious that someone had trained him to defend himself. He slammed his heel on the man's foot, then jammed his elbow into the man's gut. The man let him go before he could do more damage, and Tali stumbled forward. Julian reached for him, but unfortunately, the man grabbed him again and pulled him back. He had a gun, and he pressed it against Tali's temple.

"Don't move, neither of you," the man ordered.

They both obeyed. There was nothing Julian could do right now, and neither could Tali.

Julian raised both his hands. "Do you want money? I'll give you my wallet."

The man laughed, but it wasn't a nice sound. "I don't care about your money."

"What do you want, then? We don't have anything else."

"You."

Realization flooded Julian. "You're here because of the Family."

The man grinned. "Got it in one. Well, in two. You're going to come with me, and if you're good boy, I'll let him go."

Julian bristled at being called a boy, but there was nothing he could do about it. The man had all the power right now.

Julian had thought he and Tali would be safe, since he hadn't left the village since he'd arrived, but he'd obviously been wrong. He didn't know how the Family had managed to find him, but he did know that he'd put Tali in danger. It was his fault that Tali was in that man's hands. It was his fault that he was risking his life

Julian should have known better. He'd allowed himself to hope that everything would be okay and to forget there was someone after him for a few hours. He shouldn't have. He'd known the Family was dangerous, and he'd delivered Tali into their hands.

"I'll do everything you want if you let him go. Take me instead," he said.

The man laughed again. "That's what I was going to do anyway. Move toward me slowly."

Julian obeyed. He didn't move too close, though. He didn't want to spook the guy by moving too fast, but he also knew that if he went with him, it would be over. There was no way for him to know that the man would really let Tali go, and he couldn't risk that. He couldn't risk the man grabbing both him and Tali and taking them away. He didn't care if the Family tortured and killed him, but he wouldn't let them touch Tali. Tali was his mate, but even if he wasn't, it was Julian's duty to protect him, which sounded weird coming from a professional assassin, but it was true.

Julian didn't know what to do. He had to think coldly, but he couldn't, not when his mate was being held at gunpoint.

Tali was terrified. There was no other word for it, but he knew he had to work through that feeling.

He was scared, but he wasn't helpless.

Both the tribe and the council assassins had trained him. He might not be as good as most of them, but he could do something about the situation. He was anxious about the gun possibly going off at any second, but he knew that if he allowed Julian to give himself up, he would never see him again.

He couldn't allow that to happen.

He could see the emotion in Julian's eyes. Julian thought this was his fault, that he'd put Tali in danger, and he would never forgive himself if something happened. Well, neither would Tali. Julian had no fault in this. Even though he'd killed the head of the Family and they were now coming after him because of it, he'd done the world a favor. Tali had done some research when he'd found out about it, and he'd been horrified by what he found out. The man had been a monster of the worst species, and he was glad Julian had rid the world of him.

That didn't help their current situation, though.

He had to get away from the man holding him, and he had to do it before Julian agreed to give himself up. They both knew that there wasn't a guarantee the man would let Tali go even if he did. But even if he did let Tali go, Tali would never see Julian again. If the man managed to grab Julian and leave, that would be it. Julian wouldn't come back, and the thought made Tali's stomach churn even more than it already was.

He listened to them speaking, trying to find a way to get out of the situation. He couldn't do what he'd done earlier, not with the gun pointed at him, but he had to do *something*.

"I promise I'll give myself up, but you have to let him go first." Julian looked like he wanted to grab Tali and pull him away, but he couldn't.

"You're going to do what I say, and that's it. You don't have a choice here." The man tightened his hold on Tali, and Tali sucked in a breath.

Julian shook his head. "How do I know you're going to let him go even if I give myself up? I don't trust you."

"I don't care if you trust me or not. If you want him to live, you're coming with me."

Tali took a deep breath. He knew what he had to do, and

he was going to do it.

He waited until Julian started speaking again. Then, he shimmered away from the guy who was holding him. It only took him a few seconds. He reappeared behind him. Before the man could even realize what had happened, he grabbed the wrist of the hand that was holding the gun. He pulled it to the side so that even if the man shot, he'd hit the wall instead of Tali or Julian. Then he pushed the hand down and raised his knee to hit it.

It was a bit clumsy, but it did exactly what he'd been hoping for. The man let go of the gun as he cried out, and it fell, skittering away from him.

Tali wasn't done, though. He was angry, and he wanted the man to pay for what he was doing. Still holding the man's wrist, he twisted the guy around, then punched him straight in the face. His hand hurt with the impact, but he didn't care.

"Tali!" Julian yelled.

Tali didn't waste time to give him an explanation. He let the man go, grabbed Julian's hand, and shimmered both of them back near the village. Once they were there, he let Julian go and put his hands on his knees, holding himself up and taking a deep breath, then another. He was panting, even though he hadn't done that much, but he was freaking out.

A warm hand rubbed his back. "Tali? Are you okay?"

Tali shook his head, then nodded. He smiled when it made Julian laugh.

"That's not helping," Julian commented. "Can you speak?"

Tali straightened. "I can. I'm fine."

Julian took a step back. "You shouldn't have done that. He could have shot you."

"I had to. I had to save you."

Tali could see people rushing toward them in the distance. A few tribe members seemed to have noticed them, and they were coming to check on them. Rikar was there, and Tali wondered what was going on. Had the tribe been attacked? Was that how the Family had found Julian?

"Tali?" Rikar asked as he reached them.

Tali nodded. "I'm fine. We both are. But there's a man in an alley in town who's not. I don't know how badly I hurt him, although I doubt it was too bad. He attacked us, though. He held me at gunpoint and tried to convince Julian to go with him."

Rikar's eyes narrowed. "I take it he didn't?"

"He was ready to give himself up to save me. I stopped him before he could."

"I'll send someone into town to check. I don't like the thought of those people being around my town."

Tali agreed. "I don't understand how they found Julian. It shouldn't have been possible." The village was isolated and shielded. Nix couldn't shimmer anywhere inside the village, and there was no way for Julian to be linked to the tribe. How had the Family found out where he was? They'd been so careful. It didn't make sense.

"I don't know, but something is going on," Rikar said. He looked at Julian. "Is it possible they're tracking you through your clothes or any kind of object you've been carrying with you?"

Julian looked nonplussed. "I honestly don't know. I mean, I have clothes with me that I had before. I didn't exactly stop to buy new ones."

"You need to check everything. They might have a tracker on you, and if that's the case, they'll find you anywhere you go."

"It would make sense if they did," Tali said. "They've been finding you everywhere you go, haven't they?"

"They have, but if they do have a tracker on me, they would have found me in the warehouse, too."

"Maybe they did. Once you got to the warehouse, you

didn't leave, and they couldn't come in, just like they can't come into the village. How did they get that tracker on you, though?"

"When they caught me in the beginning. I didn't know they were looking for me, and they grabbed me. I escaped, though."

Tali nodded. "And even in Gillham, you didn't leave pack territory, and with everything going on there, security's been tightened. No person who doesn't belong would have been able to come in, and they couldn't shimmer in, either. The walk through town was the first time you made yourself vulnerable." Tali felt horrible.

He hadn't been the one who had the idea of going on a date, but he *had* agreed. Tali should have told Julian it was too dangerous. Instead, he'd been thinking about himself and how he wanted to spend time with Julian, and now, he felt guilty.

Julian reached for him. They wrapped around each other, and Tali forced himself to relax. It had been close, but they were both okay.

"It wasn't your fault," Julian murmured. "I shouldn't have agreed to go into town. I shouldn't have suggested it in the first place, but Emelie said that you enjoyed it, and I wanted to do something nice for you."

"It won't be nice if you get killed," Tali pointed out. He leaned back and looked Julian in the eyes. "But it wasn't your fault. We both knew it could be dangerous, yet we went. We should have thought about a tracker sooner. Now that we did, we need to check you out."

"I agree. We'll go over my clothes and everything I brought with me first."

They both knew the tracker would be on him, though. The man in the alley had found them too easily. If Julian had a tracker, it was on his body or the clothes he had on right now.

CHAPTER FIVE

Julian and Tali shimmered back to Gillham once they'd gone through all of Julian's things. They hadn't found the tracker there, which meant it was in Julian's body, and Julian was *pissed*.

How the Family always found him made sense now. They'd probably known where the warehouse was, too, but they hadn't been able to get inside. The same went for the Gillham pack territory and the village. As soon as Julian left one of those places, though, they'd tried to grab him, and even though it hadn't worked, Julian couldn't stop thinking about the way that man in the alley had held Tali. One of them could have been hurt, or worse, and he needed to stop thinking about it before he decided to go out and face the Family.

Now wasn't the time, not with everything going on. He had to wait a little longer, although it was tempting to leave everything behind and deal with them. But Julian knew that on his own, he wouldn't be able to do anything. He was only one man, and he needed the support of the council assassins.

Rocco met them at the infirmary. He looked puzzled, since Tali hadn't explained what they needed when he'd called. He'd just asked Rocco to be there, and of course, Rocco agreed. That was how the assassins did things.

"Tali, Julian. Everything okay?" he asked.

Julian shook his head. "Everything is *not* okay. You have to take that thing out of me."

Rocco cocked his head. "That would be easier to do if I knew what that *thing* was."

Julian sighed. "I'll explain."

"Good. I have to say I'm a little worried."

"Neither of us is wounded," Tali said. "Sorry. I should have told you when I called you, but I was freaking out."

Rocco led them inside the infirmary. Jolyn was there, too, and he rushed to Tali's side. "Rocco told me you needed us. Are you okay? Are you hurt?"

"I'm fine. We both are," Tali reassured his brother.

Julian hopped onto one of the beds. He had no idea where the tracker was in his body, and he wasn't looking forward to having people touch him to find out. Maybe they could find it another way, but he didn't want to go to the hospital to get a scan or anything like that. He would be too vulnerable.

"We know how the Family finds Julian every time he moves," Tali said. He looked at Julian, waiting for him to talk.

Julian rubbed his face. He didn't want to have to think about this, but the sooner they got the tracker out, the better it would be for everyone, especially him. "In the beginning, before I figured out someone was after me, the Family caught me," he started.

Before he could say anything else, the infirmary door opened, and Roark stepped in. Julian groaned. "Do I really have to do this in front of him?" he asked.

Roark didn't seem offended. "It's either that, or I'm listening through the window," Roark said. "What's going on?"

Julian started from the beginning again. "When I didn't know someone was after me, I got caught. I had no idea who took me, but they beat me up pretty badly. It took me a while to heal, and I hid while I did."

"Where?" Tali asked. "And why didn't they pick you up again while you were vulnerable?"

"I don't know. Maybe they were distracted or worried about the changes in the Family. Luciano wasn't the only one who wanted to take his father's place. Besides, I stayed in my rabbit form, so they might not have found me, since I don't think they were looking for a rabbit shifter. Anyway, they beat me up, and I managed to escape. Since then, they've found me everywhere I went. I didn't know who they were, and I couldn't stop to find out. I can't believe I never thought of this." Julian raked a hand through his hair. "Tali and I think they have a tracker chip in me or something like that. It's the only thing that makes sense."

Roark stared at Julian. "What happened today? What triggered all of this?"

"Tali and I left the village. We went on a date in the nearest town. One of the Family's men found us and held us at gunpoint. We managed to escape, but the only thing that makes sense in this situation is that the family has a tracker in me. How else would they be able to find me every time I leave a secure location?"

Roark's expression turned pensive. "So either the tracker doesn't work when you're in a place with Nix shields in place like the warehouse or pack territory, or it does work, but they don't attack you because it's dangerous for them."

"Exactly." Julian didn't know which option was correct, but he didn't think it mattered. The fact that the family might have been right outside the warehouse waiting for him to leave was kind of creepy, though.

"Well, it depends on what kind of technology the tracker uses," Rocco said. "Either option is possible."

Julian shook his head. "I don't care what technology the tracker uses. I just wanted it out of me."

Roark nodded. "Of course. What I meant is that depending on what kind of technology the tracker uses, we could shimmer you to a hospital to get a full-body scan."

"I can't risk it. Can you check me?" Julian asked Rocco.

"I can, but I don't know how useful it's going to be. I'll try, but it depends on how big the tracker is and where it's positioned." He looked at the other three men in the room. "We'll start with the places anyone can touch. Roark, I think Julian would be more comfortable if you stepped out. Tali, Jolyn. Care to help me?"

Julian didn't want anyone but Tali touching his body, but he knew better than to suggest that. Having three people looking for it would be faster.

Rocco turned toward him. "Take everything but your pants and underwear off. We'll start with that, and if we don't find the tracker, you'll remove those clothes, too. Unless you've felt something strange anywhere? Maybe when you showered?"

"I haven't. I doubt it's under my pants, though. They never removed them when they beat me up."

Rocco's lips quirked into a smile. "Good for you. You won't have to get naked in front of us, then."

Jolyn made a retching sound. "I don't want to see my brother's mate naked."

"Well, since you're a healer, you might have to one day, but we don't have to think about that now," Rocco said, still smiling.

Julian relaxed. He still wasn't comfortable with knowing he had a tracker inside his body, but Rocco's behavior was helping. Julian was pissed, yes, but there was nothing else he could do right now, so he obeyed Rocco's order and took off his clothes. Rocco had him stay on the bed, while he, Tali, and Jolyn ran their fingertips over his chest and shoulders.

Julian jerked when someone — he couldn't see who because they were behind him — pressed against his side. "Don't touch that spot," he said.

Tali appeared in Julian's sight. "You're ticklish?"

"I'm not. I just don't like being touched there." At least it was Tali and not one of the other two.

"You're ticklish, then. Good to know."

The way he said it made Julian want to grab him and drag him to the closest bed, but he stayed right where he was. Maybe it wasn't good that Tai had been the one to touch him there after all.

"I think I found something," Jolyn said. He was working on the back of Julian's neck.

Rocco and Tali joined him so they could see what he was talking about, leaving Julian facing forward alone.

"I think that's it," Jolyn said, pushing a spot on Julian's neck.

"It looks like it," Rocco agreed. He touched the spot, too, and Julian started feeling like too many people were touching him.

"I'll take it out of you right now," Rocco said. "It's going to hurt a bit, but Tali will heal you right away."

"Just take it out," Julian snapped. He wasn't angry at Rocco, but he wanted that thing out of his body. Knowing it was there made him feel weird.

There was a flash of pain, then Julian felt blood trickling down his neck. He didn't know how the Family had managed to put the tracker there. From what he knew, usually, this kind of tracker was put in the arm. Maybe they'd used the back of his neck so he wouldn't find it, and they'd been right. He hadn't known anything about the tracker until Rikar had suggested it.

Rocco walked around Julian while Tali gently cupped the back of his neck with his hand. "Here it is," Rocco said, holding out a metal bowl.

Julian stared at the bit of metal. Now that it was out of him, what were they going to do with it?

The thought of having a tracker inside his body made Tali's skin crawl, and he hadn't even been the one to have it inside him. He didn't understand how Julian wasn't pushing that thing away while screaming in horror. He would have in his place.

"Well, look at that," Roark said as he walked back in. He didn't sound worried, which surprised Tali a bit.

"What are you going to do with it?" Julian asked.

"I'll talk to Win and Kameron, but I think it would be best if it were destroyed."

"At least the Family can't find me anymore."

Tali wanted to believe that. "They already know you're in Gillham, though," he pointed out.

"But if I go, they won't be able to follow me. They might find me again one day, but in the meantime, you'll be safe."

Tali knew Julian wouldn't back down. The best way to be free of the Family was to get rid of them, not to run away from them, and eventually, Julian would face them. Tali didn't like that thought, but there was nothing he could do about it. He wanted to keep Julian wrapped in cotton and away from the world, but Julian was a strong man, and he would do whatever he wanted. He and Tali weren't even bonded, for fuck's sake. Tali didn't even know if it was something Julian might want. So far, the only thing he did know was that Julian was free and that he might leave. He didn't like the thought, especially since Julian had promised he wasn't going anywhere, but was there anything Tali could do if it happened?

"I want to use the tracker to set up a trap," Julian said, looking at Roark.

Roark's eyebrows climbed high on his forehead. "A trap?"

"I don't want to spend the rest of my life running from the Family. I can hope they'll lose interest in me eventually, but I don't want to rely on that. I want to be able to stop looking over my shoulder every single second." He looked at Tali. "I want people to be safe around me, or as safe as possible anyway." He turned his attention back to Roark. "I know I can't make this kind of decision if I want your help, but I think a trap would be a good idea."

Roark took a few seconds to think about it. "I can certainly bring it up to the council, and of course, to Win. I can't make that decision, but I do know that all the assassins will be on board. You're one of us now, and we'll keep you safe."

Julian's expression twisted, and Tali found himself reaching for him. He knew how much those words meant to his mate. From what he knew, Julian had his own family, but he fit in perfectly with the assassins, just like Tali did. They were both pulled in two different directions when it came to families, but that was one of the greatest problems to have. Having two families was better than having none, especially when they were as great as Tali's were. He could only hope the same went for Julian.

"Let me make a few phone calls," Roark said. "I'll let you know as soon as I can."

"I'm going to continue checking Julian, just in case," Rocco said. "I doubt two trackers were used, but I want to be sure just in case."

Julian groaned. "You're not done touching me?"

Rocco laughed. "No, but we can have Tali do it if you want."

Julian held his hands out. "Fine. Do your worst."

This time, Tali stayed in front of Julian. He could feel how uncomfortable Julian was with Rocco and Jolyn touching him, and he tried to distract him, gently stroking his cheeks, keeping his attention on him. He wasn't sure it worked, but once Rocco and Jolyn were done, he and Julian headed to the bathroom.

"I'm sorry, but I'm not letting anyone other than you touch me in places only you should be touching," Julian said as they walked in.

Tali was pretty sure his cheeks were red, but he ignored

everything that wasn't Julian taking off his pants. He still had his underwear on, and when he reached for them, Tali stopped him by touching his arm. "I don't think it's necessary for you to take those off. The cotton is thin enough that I should be able to feel a tracker through it."

Julian's smile was cheeky. "Are you sure? Don't you want me naked?"

Tali's cheeks were on fire. "Not in this situation, no. We can talk about it later, though."

Julian stared for a moment. "I think I like that idea." He licked his lips. "I know we haven't talked about what we want much."

"I don't know if we need to do that now." Tali didn't want Julian to make any kind of promises.

He had no idea what would happen once the Family had been taken care of. Julian had promised he would stick around, but would he really? Tali didn't want to think about it. He only wanted to focus on Julian.

He touched every single inch of Julian's legs, looking for a tracker, but also memorizing him. He didn't know if he'd ever get the chance to touch him this way again. He wanted to believe he would, but if Julian left, Tali wouldn't go with him. They should talk about it, but Tali couldn't, not when he was aware of the fact that Julian himself didn't know what was next. Maybe he would stay with them once the Family had been taken care of, or maybe he would go back to his life before all that happened. There was no way for anyone to know until he got rid of the Family, and Tali wasn't going to ask.

"I didn't find anything," he said. "I'm going to step out. You should check between your legs."

"You don't want to do that for me?"

Tali wanted to do it more than anything right now, even though the situation was less than ideal. Still, he shook his head. "Not here."

Julian nodded. "I'll check. Thank you."

Tali slipped out of the bathroom only to find that Roark had come back.

"Everything okay in there?" Roark asked.

Tali looked away as he walked closer. "I didn't find anything else on him, so I think there was only one tracker."

"Good."

The door opened behind Tali, and he heard Julian move toward them. "Well?" Julian asked

"The council agreed. Well, the part of the council Kameron managed to reach. He said he would call the other members and tell them what's going on, but he doesn't think it will be a problem. He just needs a majority. I also called Win, and he gave us the go-ahead, so we can start planning the trap you want to put in place."

Julian's expression lightened, and for a moment, he looked like a kid in a candy store. "Great. Well, I don't think it should be too complicated. They're waiting for me to leave one of my safe places, so we could probably go back to the warehouse, but maybe stay out of it? That way, there won't be a lot of people around. The assassins who want to help can wait inside for the Family to arrive and grab them."

"That sounds good, but we need to go into more details," Roark said.

Tali listened to them talk for a few seconds, but he couldn't stay for long. He couldn't stand hearing that stuff. It could mean Julian would leave him behind, and he wasn't strong enough to deal with it right now.

He snuck out of the room without anyone seeing he was leaving, or at least, he thought so. His brother noticed, of course, and he was right behind him. "Are you okay?" Jolyn asked.

"I'll be better once this situation is over."

"You think he's going to leave?"

"I don't know." And that was even more terrifying than when the man in the alley had dragged him away.

Julian had noticed Tali leaving, and he didn't know why. He wanted to go to Tali and ask him, but he had to focus on keeping himself and everyone else safe, which meant that he couldn't back down when it came to the trap.

It was a good idea. Even Roark had approved, which meant that sooner rather than later, Julian would be rid of the Family. That had been his goal since they'd started hunting him, and he couldn't wait to be free again. He wanted to be able to take Tali on a date without one of them being held at gunpoint. He wanted to be free to leave the Gillham pack territory or the warehouse without worrying whether or not he would come back in one piece.

He didn't know how he would get rid of the Family yet, but the *how* didn't matter.

Maybe Tali was just talking to his brother. Jolyn had followed him outside, so it was possible. There might be more to it, but Julian would have to wait before talking to him. He wanted Tali's approval when it came to this plan, but he would go ahead with it even if he didn't have it.

"I think it'll work," Roark agreed.

"Can you call the assassins and see who wants in?" Julian asked.

"Of course. I'm pretty sure everyone will want to help, but it doesn't mean they'll be able to. I'll call and ask, though. When do you want to do it?"

Julian bit his lower lip as he thought. His instinct was to say right away, but he knew they had to get ready first. "As soon as possible. When do you think everything will be ready?"

"Well, there's not a lot to do. I have to contact everyone and check with them, and of course, we have to decide who is going to hide where, but that's about it." Roark paused. "You also have to decide what you're going to do once you get your hands on those guys. I doubt the head of the Family is going to try to get to you himself."

"Definitely not. He's going to send someone to pick me up, and he's probably going to want to torture me before killing me."

"That means we have to go to him."

Julian cracked his knuckles. "We can use whoever he sends. They won't willingly go along with the plan, but if we threaten them, it probably won't be a problem. Or maybe we can use Armand. He could shift into that person, and we can face the head of the Family that way."

"Armand will be going with you regardless. I don't want you to go alone. The other assassins would have a harder time following you, but a few of us could use our powers to sneak in. I'll have to think about it, but it's definitely possible."

Julian was touched. He was pretty sure that only six months ago, Roark would have gladly allowed the Family to take him. Hell, he would have delivered him himself. Things were different now, though, and Julian wasn't alone anymore.

"Okay. So we'll catch the person who comes to pick me up at the warehouse, and then we'll convince him or her to take us back to the Family. Once we manage that, Armand will come with me shifted into that person. You said others might be able to come along?"

"You can probably carry at least Lawrence in his shifted form on you. He's a snake."

Julian grimaced. "I'm not looking forward to going around with a snake in my pocket, but sure. Why not? Anyone else?"

"Evan. He's a chameleon shifter, so he's small, too, and he can be invisible. Maybe even Miles. He can manipulate his body, but I don't know how small he can make it. I'll ask him.

I've never been on a mission with him, so I've never seen him do his thing on the job."

"You think they'll all want to come along?"

"If they can, yes. Honestly, I'd like to come with you, too, but you can't exactly fit me in your pocket."

Julian barked out a laugh. "That would be a sight."

"I *could* use my power, though." Roark hummed as he thought. "Yes, I like that."

Julian liked it, too. "All right. We have a basic plan. We can't move forward until you know who's up for it, so I'll wait until you talk to everyone to make decisions."

Roark nodded. "Good. And you should go after your mate. It's obvious something is up with him."

Julian hesitated, but he couldn't ask anyone else right now. "What do you think is going on with him?"

Roark shrugged. "No idea. Did something happen while you were at the village?"

"Well, we *were* held at gunpoint." It was entirely possible that that was the reason Tali had left. Maybe he didn't want to listen to this kind of conversation because it reminded him of that.

Roark grimaced. "I doubt that made things easy for him. Talk to him. It's the best way to solve things when you're in a relationship. I know it's not easy, but that way you'll know what's going on instead of guessing."

He was right. If he and Tali wanted to make a go at a relationship and for things to work between them, they had to talk and make sure that neither of them made big decisions without the other knowing about it.

Maybe that was a problem. Maybe Tali didn't want Julian to do this. Julian didn't know what he would do if that was the case, but he decided not to think about it before he talked to Tali. "I'll talk to him," he told Roark. "Thanks for the help. I don't know what I would do if I didn't have you and the other assassins."

"You'd already be dead," Roark said, humor his voice.

Julian couldn't deny that, no matter how little he liked it. "Let me know as soon as you hear from the others. If we can, I think I'd like to do this sometime over the next few days."

"I'll tell everyone that. In the meantime, you should carry the tracker with you. Otherwise, the Family will realize it's not moving and that you found it. No one's going to believe that you're sticking to one place for several days."

Julian hadn't thought of that, and he was glad Roark had.

He waited for Rocco to clean the tracker, then, he put it in his pocket. It was in a small plastic baggie so that he wouldn't lose it.

Once he had it, he headed home. Tali and Jolyn were nowhere to be seen when he left the infirmary, so he thought that was where he'd find them. He hoped so, anyway. He didn't know what was going on with Tali, but he needed to find out before the trap happened. He didn't want to leave Tali behind without knowing what was going on between them.

Julian had thought they were making progress, but now he wasn't so sure anymore. Was there a problem? Had Tali changed his mind? Maybe it was too much for him. Julian couldn't say he'd blame him if that was the case. It was too much even for him, but he couldn't exactly ignore the situation.

When he got home, Ox and Cam were in the living room watching a movie. Since Tali wasn't there, Julian didn't stop to chat. He headed upstairs to the room Tali and his brother shared and knocked on the door.

The door swung open. Jolyn stood there, staring at Julian. Julian wasn't sure how he knew that Jolyn was standing in front of him rather than Tali. The two were identical twins.

But Julian didn't feel as drawn to Jolyn as he did to Tali. It was odd, but it was a sure way for him to know who was Tali and who was Jolyn.

Jolyn looked back. "I'm going downstairs," he said.

"Sure," Tali said, but he sounded reluctant.

Jolyn stepped out in the hallway. "Be good to him," he murmured as he passed by Julian.

"Always," Julian answered. Then he stepped into the bedroom, closing the door behind himself. "I know you're worried," he began when Tali didn't say anything. "I'm sorry. If I had a choice, I wouldn't do this, but I have to. I have to keep everyone safe, and that includes you. I don't know what else to tell you. I wish you didn't have to deal with this, but I—" Julian sucked in a breath. He didn't know what else to say.

Tali rose from the window seat and came closer. "I know you have to do it. I won't try to stop you."

"Then you understand. I have to get rid of the Family, or at the very least, to make sure they'll stop hunting me. I want to be able to be with you without being afraid someone will find us and hurt you. I don't want to put you in danger. I already did, and it was horrible. I don't know what I would have done if that man had shot you."

Julian prayed Tali would understand. He truly didn't know what he would do if that wasn't the case.

To his relief, Tali reached up with both hands and cupped Julian's face. "I understand all of that, Julian. I don't like it, but I know it's the only way to change this situation and for you to be free."

"Are you sure?"

In response, Tali leaned closer and kissed Julian.

Tali didn't want Julian to do it. It was dangerous, and the only thing he could think about was that Julian would get hurt.

Julian was right, though. If he didn't do it, he would have to run for the rest of his life, or at the very least, for several years. Tali would have to choose between Julian and the assassins, and he didn't want to. He might still have to if Julian decided to leave once he was rid of the Family, but it wasn't something Tali wanted to talk about right now.

So he kissed Julian, pressing their lips together for the first time. Julian stayed frozen for a moment, but Tali didn't move away. He knew Julian wanted this as much as he did. He wanted Julian, and Julian wanted him. He didn't know when the trap was supposed to happen, but he didn't want to waste the little time he had with his mate.

He relaxed when Julian wrapped his arms around him. He'd been sure Julian wanted this, but he felt better having a sign of it. Julian was kissing him back, gently pressing his lips with his tongue, and Tali opened up to him. He lost himself in the kiss, and it was better than obsessing over what was going to happen next.

"I'm never leaving you," Julian murmured. "If I have a choice, I'm never leaving you,"

Tali squeezed his eyes shut. "Not even once you get rid of the Family?" He hadn't wanted to ask, but Julian had brought it up, and now, Tali wanted to know.

"Not even then. The only way you're getting rid of me is by telling me you don't want me. I'm not going anywhere, Tali. I have to do this because I can't spend my life waiting for the Family to catch up to me, but once it's done, I'll be able to focus on you and our future. I want you in my life. I've never wanted anyone as much as I want you, and that's not going to change anytime soon."

Tali wanted to believe it, and maybe he did. It didn't matter anyway. Julian had probably had other people in his life, but Tali was his mate, and *that* was the only thing that mattered.

He kissed Julian again, needing to be closer to him. He

wanted so much more, but he didn't know how to ask for it.

"What do you want?" Julian asked, because of course he did.

"I don't know. Anything. Everything."

Julian chuckled. "You can have anything you want from me. I promise."

Tali had to take a step back because he was scared of the first thing that popped into his mind when Julian said those words. "Anything?" he asked.

"Anything. It doesn't matter what you ask. I'll always try to give it to you."

"Then I want us to bond," Tali said before he could think better of it.

To his surprise, Julian didn't say no right away. Instead, he asked, "Can I ask why you want to bond with me?"

"Because we're mates."

"And? I'm pretty sure it's not the only reason."

"I know you're going to do this whether or not I like it, and I understand why. I want us to be bonded so that if something happens, you can contact me. I want you to be able to talk to me and tell me what's going on. I know I won't be there. I'm not a council assassin, and even though I can defend myself, I'm not a fighter."

Julian laughed. "I'm pretty sure the guy you beat up doesn't agree with that."

"You know what I mean. I can't help you when you go take care of the Family, but this, I can do."

"All right. Let's do it."

Tali blinked. He'd expected Julian to protest. "That easily?"

"Did you want me to say no? Because I can, even though I don't want to."

"Do you think this is the wrong reason to bond?"

"Maybe. Doesn't matter, though. We already know we're going to end up together. You're my mate, and I want everything with you, just like you want everything with me. Maybe it's too soon for us to bond, but I don't see why that should stop us. I want to be one with you, and I think it would be a good thing if you were able to hear my thoughts when I face the Family. I don't want you there, but you'll be there with me through our bond."

Tali reached for him. Julian came, and Tali curled himself around him as best as he could. He pressed his ear against Julian's chest, listening to his heart beating. "I'll always be with you once we bond. You just have to talk to me, and I'll hear you." He would always be there for Julian, whatever happened.

"And knowing this would make you feel better about the plan, right?"

"It would. I don't like the thought that I can't go with you, but I know it's for the best. This way, I'll still be with you."

"Let's do it, then."

Tali didn't only want to bond, though. He couldn't think about the fact that this might be the last few days they had together, but he did know that if they bonded, he wanted everything that went with it. And once they were together, no one would be able to separate them.

He wanted to make love with Julian. Julian might have a family, but Tali knew he'd been alone a long time, especially after he'd started running from the Family. He hadn't believed he could turn to anyone for help, and he'd been wrong. Tali wanted to show him just *how* wrong he'd been. He wanted Julian to feel cherished and loved, and he wasn't sure how to do that except through his actions. It was too soon to say the words out loud, but eventually, they would tell each other.

He tilted his face up, and they kissed again. It was soft, gentle, at least for a bit. Tali knew it wouldn't last, though. He wanted Julian too fiercely.

He reached for the bottom of Julian's t-shirt, struggling to haul it up. It made Julian chuckle, and he finally stepped away, raising his arms.

Tali got rid of his t-shirt, throwing it to the floor. Then he reached for Julian's jeans.

"What will your brother say about this?" Julian asked.

Tali froze. "Why are you talking about Jolyn right now?"

"There's only one bed in here. I know you've been sharing. Will he have anything to say about us having sex on it?"

"I don't know. He can move into your room while you move in here with me if it makes him feel better, though." That sounded like a good idea, regardless.

Julian nodded, apparently placated.

Tali opened Julian's jeans and pushed them to his feet. Then he hooked his fingers into Julian's underwear and looked up. "Still sure you want this?"

"I've never been surer of anything."

Tali pushed those down, too. Since Julian was wearing his shoes and socks, he was stuck where he was. He didn't have to be stuck for long. Tali knelt in front of him and reached for one of his feet. He gently took the shoe and sock away. Then he wriggled Julian's jeans and underwear off. Once that was done, he turned his attention to the other foot.

Finally Julian was standing naked in front of him. He was glorious, and Tali couldn't resist—he leaned forward and pressed a kiss to the tip of Julian's cock.

It twitched. Tali looked up, wondering what now. Julian was staring down at him with hooded eyes, and Tali opened his mouth, wrapping his lips around Julian's cock. Since Julian didn't push him away, Tali sucked.

Strong fingers dug into his hair. He closed his eyes, because he couldn't stand the tension between him and Julian as they stared at each other while he blew him. It made him want to strip and jump onto Julian's cock, but instead, he focused on what he was doing. He wanted Julian to feel loved, and this was one of the ways to make that happen.

He wrapped his hands around the back of Julian's thighs so he could hold him close and took care of his cock. He licked the shaft, taking his time learning every single inch of skin. Julian smelled good, like soap and man, like he was Tali's.

And he was. They were becoming one, and Tali couldn't have been happier.

"I want to touch you, too," Julian murmured.

"You are," Tali said as he let go of Julian's cock.

"I want to do more, though. I want to be inside you. That's something you want, too?"

"I do." But for that, Tali would have to get naked.

He held a hand up, and Julian helped him to his feet. Then Tali reached for his t-shirt. Before he could grab it, though, Julian stopped him with a hand on his wrist. "Let me," he murmured.

Tali swallowed and nodded. He raised his hands, and Julian slowly pulled his t-shirt off. It was excruciating, because every inch of fabric that left Tali's body was replaced by the touch of Julian's fingers. They brushed against him, lightly touching his stomach, his chest, his nipples. Julian was obviously being slow on purpose, but Tali wasn't about to ask him to stop.

It became even worse once Julian reached for Tali's jeans. He moved as slowly as he had before, touching every inch of Tali's legs. He stroked his fingertips around Tali's waist, then down to his ass. He didn't continue the way Tali wanted. Instead, he moved them down to his thighs. The jeans went, along with Tali's underwear, and then Tali was in the same position Julian had been earlier. He was stuck with his shoes on. Julian did as Tali had before, kneeling in front of him and getting rid of them. Then they were both naked, and Tali waited.

Julian got back to his feet and gently steered Tali toward the bed. "I'm going to need some lube."

Tali gestured toward the dresser. "First drawer on the right."

Julian nodded, but he didn't say anything. Instead, he moved toward the dresser.

Tali stretched out on the bed. He opened his legs, sucked a finger into his mouth, then reached for his hole. By the time Julian turned around, he already had it deep inside him.

Julian arched a brow when he saw him. "Impatient?"

"I wanted this the first time I saw you. Hell, yes, I'm impatient. Come here."

Julian obeyed. Tali took his finger out of his body and held it out, and Julian opened the lube. He slicked Tali's fingers, and Tali went back to prepping himself for his mate.

Of course, Julian wasn't about to let that happen without getting involved. He slicked his own fingers. Once Tali had two of his own inside his body, Julian added one of his.

It made Tali feel full, but the stretch was delicious. He wanted Julian's cock desperately, so he rushed through prepping himself. Julian was taking things much slower, toying with Tali's body until it made Tali feel like he was about to explode.

Luckily for everyone, he didn't. Once both he and Julian had two fingers inside of him, he decided he was ready. His cock was hard, so hard he could pound nails with it, and Julian's was leaking. He was as ready as Tali to take the next step, and when Tali took his fingers out of his ass, so did Julian.

He settled between Tali's legs and looked down at him. "Still sure you want this?" he asked.

"I am, and I'm also sure I want you to stop asking. Come on, Julian. I want you, and I want to bond with you. Make it happen."

Julian chuckled and obeyed. He grabbed his cock and aimed it toward Tali's hole, and Tali held his breath.

It hurt a bit in the beginning, but it wouldn't forever. Besides, he wanted Julian inside of him more than he cared about the pain.

Julian was still slow and careful, though. He kept kissing Tali, going from his mouth to his cheeks, to his neck, only to go back to his lips. Tali wanted him to hurry, but he understood why Julian wasn't.

Instead of asking him to, he waited. Once Julian was fully inside of him, though, his patience broke. He looked at Julian, then, still staring him in the eyes, he pressed a hand against Julian's chest. "Is this where you want my mark?" he asked.

Julian nodded. "As long as I can mark you while you do it."

Tali tilted his head to the side. Julian moved closer until Tali was slightly uncomfortable with his arm scrunched up the way it was, but he didn't care. It was a position in which they would claim each other, and it was perfect.

It hurt when Julian bit him, but only for a second. Julian started moving his hips as soon as blood spurted out of the wound, and everything turned to pleasure. There was no pain anymore, nowhere in Tali's body. There was only pleasure, and he felt his orgasm rise even though he wanted this to last. He couldn't think anymore, his body taking charge. He yearned to bond with Julian, and his body seemed to be okay with that.

Julian moved quickly and hard into Tali's body as he drank down Tali's blood. Tali's hand was so hot that it hurt, but Julian didn't say anything, and it had to be worse for him. Instead, he continued to fuck Tali until they both felt the bond snap into place between them.

Tali cried out, throwing his head back and dislodging Julian's mouth from his neck. That was okay, though. The bond was in place, and Julian continued licking Tali's neck as he continued fucking him.

Pleasure rose in Tali, and now that he could feel Julian's, too, it was overwhelming. He didn't even try to stop his orgasm when he felt it. He knew he wouldn't be able to, not with Julian moving inside him and around him, with the bond making a loop between their pleasures.

He came, and Julian stiffened on top of him. From the feeling through the bond, he was pretty sure Julian was coming, too. He doubted coming at the same time was something that happened often, and he knew it made their bonding special.

Julian relaxed. Then, he rolled to his side, taking Tali with him. His cock slid out of Tali, leaving him feeling empty, but he snuggled against his mate's chest. He liked that they didn't have to talk to be able to communicate. He liked that on Julian's chest, his mark stood out starkly, both their initials intertwined. It would be there forever, just like Julian's bite would be on Tali's neck.

Whatever happened, they would always be together, and if Julian needed him, Tali would come to the rescue.

CHAPTER SIX

"Ready?"

Julian *wasn't* ready, but he still nodded at Dasha. Dasha held his hand out, and Julian took it. They shimmered to the warehouse, where some of the other assassins were already standing, looking at each other and probably wondering what the next step was. They were supposed to know, and Julian glared at them. "Go inside," he snapped. "You were supposed to be inside by the time I got here."

Armand rolled his eyes at him, but they all obeyed.

Not all of them were there, even though they'd wanted to be. Julian had received several messages from those who were busy or away, and he'd been touched. He hadn't expected all of them to want to be there for him, and it was a strange feeling.

The ones who *were* there would be useful, though. Julian already knew they would help him as much as they could, even though he didn't fully understand why they'd wanted to be present.

Arrived? Tali asked through their mental bond.

It was still strange to hear him in his mind this way, but Julian was getting used to it, and it was the only reason Tali had agreed to stay back at the Gillham pack. *Arrived*, he confirmed.

Let me know if anything happens.

I will. Don't worry too much, though.

Don't worry too much? You're kidding, right?

Julian didn't know how to answer that. He didn't want Tali

93

to worry, but he understood why that wasn't possible. *I'll be careful.*

The problem is that I don't know if it will be enough. Come back to me in one piece, Julian. We haven't had enough time together yet.

I agree. I promise to be careful.

I'm keeping you to that promise. Now go. The sooner you do this, the sooner you'll be back. Besides, if the Family is keeping an eye on you, they probably know where you are now.

Julian turned his attention to what was around him rather than the bond. They'd all crowded into the warehouse, but they hadn't left the stairs. The place wasn't as secure as it used to be, even though the security system was back in place. People knew where it was now, so it would be dangerous for anyone to move back in here.

That wasn't what they were doing anyway.

Even Win was there, and he looked worried. They all turned to him since he was their boss, but he gestured at Roark and Julian, who were standing next to each other. "Don't look at me. They're the ones doing this, so refer to them today."

It was daunting to have every eye on him, but Julian cleared his throat and nodded. "You already know the plan. I'm going to go back out there, maybe act as if I'm cleaning up." There was still some damage outside from when the warehouse had been attacked, and the broken furniture and other things had been brought outside. It would give Julian a fake reason to be there. "You're to stay inside. I don't know if the Family will believe I'm alone. So Dasha will come with me, and he'll tell me he's going back to Gillham to pick up something, or whatever. He'll shimmer away, and we'll wait. I'm hoping whoever the Family is sending will be stupid enough to believe all of this. You'll stay inside until they're here. Once they are, we'll attack. I don't know how many people will be sent, but I suspect it will be more than one considering what happened the last time they sent only one guy."

Armand snickered. "Tali kicked his ass, that's what happened."

The assassins had been impressed with how Tali had defended himself, and Tali had glowed under their praise. It had been good to see, and Julian was glad the assassins loved Tali. He'd known it, of course, but it was still strange to have such a big family of people who weren't related to him.

"Once they arrive and the fight is over—and I know we'll win—we'll have to try to find the guy in charge. Armand can turn into him, and we'll go back to the Family."

"How do you think they'll get here?" Tony asked.

Julian wasn't sure it was a good idea for Tony to be here, but Tony had insisted. Julian had saved him, and he wanted to do the same for him. He'd promised he would stay back and only act if the other assassins needed backup, which was the only reason Win had allowed him to come.

"I don't know, but I suspect they'll shimmer. It's the only way for them to get to me fast enough that I won't leave before they do."

"So there'll be a Nix with them, since they'll also have to shimmer back," Dasha pointed out.

"Either that, or they'll use a Nix service."

Armand snorted. "Can you imagine that? Let's order a Nix while we grab this guy and kidnap him."

"Maybe you can shift into the Nix rather than the guy in charge. I don't know much about the Family, even though I tried to get more information. They've become secretive since I killed the head of the Family, and the only thing I'm sure of is that his son is now in charge and trying to kill me. This is the best we could do, and you're free to go if you don't think we'll win."

Julian looked around, but from their expression, it was obvious they weren't going anywhere. He relaxed, even though the day was far from being over.

"All right. I'm going out. Dasha?"

Dasha nodded and followed Julian outside. They stood in front of the door, examining the damage. "I hadn't realized it was this bad," Julian said. "I've been here before to pick up my things, but it didn't look so bad when the furniture and everything else was inside the house."

Dasha reached out and squeezed Julian's shoulder. "Don't worry too much. No one is going to live here again. We just need to grab the stuff that can be sent to the new place."

They started working, putting the things that could be saved on one side, and the other, the stuff that had to be thrown away. There was a lot more in that pile, and it quickly grew.

"I'm going to shimmer to the grocery store and grab garbage bags," Dasha said.

He and Julian looked at each other, and Julian nodded. "Sure. I'll continue working. That way, we might be able to go home soon."

"We'll have to come back, but yeah. Good plan."

He shimmered away, leaving Julian alone. Julian went back to what he was doing, but he was very much aware of the world around him. He knew he had to be careful, but there was no way for him to know whether or not the family had decided to come and try to take him or not.

They had.

A man appeared from behind the warehouse, making enough noise that Julian heard him right away. He was followed by another two—none of them a Nix—and Julian straightened, staring at them. "Can I help you?" he asked.

"You're coming with us," the man in front growled.

Julian rolled his eyes. "Can't you see I have things to do? I'm not leaving."

The man took a gun out of his pocket. "It wasn't a suggestion. It was an order, and if you don't want me to shoot you,

you'll come with me."

Julian raised his hands and examined the other men. One was obviously uncomfortable. He kept looking around as if he expected someone to attack them, and he wasn't wrong.

The warehouse door burst open, and the assassins filed out.

The man holding a gun looked bewildered. He dropped the gun without anyone even asking.

"Well, that was boring," Armand said. "I was hoping there would be a bit more excitement."

North slapped his stomach. "Shut it. Your mate will be happy that you didn't try to get yourself killed. Think about that, huh?"

"Besides, you're still going to shift into one of these guys and take me to the Family." Julian wasn't happy about that part of the plan, but it had to be done. It was the only way this was ever going to be over.

The man who'd put the gun down moved before anyone could do anything about it, and at the same time, about a dozen men rushed from behind the warehouse toward the assassins. The man dove for his gun, and someone cried out, but he managed to shoot once before Armand tackled him. Heat and pain flashed in Julian's arm, and he swore.

He slapped his hand on his arm, and his fingers came back dirty with blood just as someone barreled into him and threw him to the ground.

Tali felt pain flash through the bond he shared with Julian, and he freaked out.

Julian? What's going on?

Julian didn't answer, which wasn't reassuring. Tali was seconds away from shimmering to the warehouse and seeing what was happening on his own, but Jolyn grabbed his wrist to keep him in place. "Wait," he said.

Tali turned to look at him. "He's hurt. I can feel it."

"I understand, but you have to wait. Whatever is happening is not good, and I don't want you to walk in on that. You could get hurt."

"Julian is already hurt!"

"Try talking to him through the bond again. He might be hurt, but he might also be busy kicking ass. Do you really want to go there and interrupt him? What do you think is going to happen if he sees you?"

Tali swallowed and had to agree that his brother wasn't wrong. Julian would be distracted if he saw Tali there, and that was the last thing Tali wanted.

Julian? he called out again.

When he had no answer, he couldn't wait anymore. He shook his brother's hand off his arm. "I'm sorry, but I have to go."

Jolyn narrowed his eyes. "Then I'm coming with you. If someone is wounded, they're going to need both of us."

Tali didn't waste time protesting. Just like he knew what he was doing, so did Jolyn.

Together, they shimmered in front of the warehouse. The first thing Tali saw was a huge man standing over Julian. He had no idea what was happening, but he could see the assassins who'd agreed to be there fighting with other guys. Julian was on the ground, his arm bleeding, but he was getting back to his feet. The man standing over him wasn't going to give him enough time to do that, though. Tali had to act, and he had to act quickly.

He shimmered again, closer this time—so close that he ended up on the guy's back, which was what he'd been trying to do. He wrapped himself around the man like a koala, holding on for dear life as the guy straightened and tried to swat him off his back.

"What the fuck?" the guy asked.

Julian's eyes were wide, but Tali only got a glimpse of him. It was too hard to hold onto the guy and focus on Julian at the same time.

Julian got to his feet, but he wasn't the first who reached Tali, and the guy who was still trying to buck him off. Tony got there first, a fierce expression on his face.

He reached out and touched the man, and Tali could feel the cold coursing through the guy. The guy froze, quite literally, and Tali had to jump off his back. He shivered, but Julian was there, wrapping his arms around him, apparently not caring about the fact that he was bleeding. "Tali? What are you doing here?"

"You're didn't answer when I tried talking to you through the bond. What did you think I would do?"

Julian shook his head. "You could have gotten hurt."

"So could you. Actually, you *got* hurt. I felt it through the bond." Tali took a step back and looked at Julian's arm. Sure enough, there was blood on his sleeve. His arm was bleeding.

Tali reached out and pressed his hand on top of the wound. He closed his eyes, focusing on it as Julian continued to scold him gently.

"You shouldn't have come. You risked a lot, and I can only imagine what would have happened if you got hurt. I would've gone crazy."

The wound wasn't bad, certainly not as bad as Tali had thought when he'd seen the blood. It appeared to be a bullet wound, but it had only brushed past Julian, and it hadn't penetrated his arm. There was a gash, yes, but that was it. Tali focused on knitting the skin back together, doing the best job he could.

"You shouldn't throw yourself into fights like that," Julian continued.

Tali opened his eyes. "I'm fine. Don't worry about me."

"You could have been hurt," Julian repeated.

"And you would have known how I felt when I felt that pain through the bond," Tali snapped. He pressed his lips together and swallowed. "I understand you're worried, but I'm fine. I needed to help you, and I did. I just healed you."

Julian pulled his t-shirt away from the wound to check it, and sure enough, under all the blood that was already drying, the skin was healed. "Thank you," he murmured. His eyes shone with something Tali couldn't identify. "I'm sorry I yelled at you. I was scared for you."

Tali nodded. "I know. I could feel that, too. I'm sure you felt as terrified as I was when I felt your pain."

Julian opened his arms, and Tali fitted himself between them. He curled himself around his mate, breathing in his scent. It was mixed with blood, but it was still Julian, and it made Tali feel better. "What happened?" he asked.

"I'm not sure. There were only three guys in the beginning, and they were easy to deal with. But then other guys came out of nowhere, and they attacked us. I was already wounded because I'd been shot, and that guy just threw me to the ground."

"You were going to kick his ass anyway, weren't you?"

Julian laughed. "Of course. I'm still grateful you intervened, though."

"I wasn't going to watch from the sideline and do nothing." Tali stepped away and looked around. The other bad guys had been subdued. Most of them were unconscious, but a few were tied up and sitting on the ground. They were complaining, and Tali had to resist the urge to go to them and kick them in the balls.

They'd attacked his mate. They'd gone to what had once been his home and fought the people he considered his family. He wanted to kick their asses, but he knew better than to try.

"I'm going to go around and check if anyone is wounded,"

he told Julian.

"That's a good idea. I'll come with you. It's my fault they're here, after all."

"You might not know them as well as I do, but I'm sure you're aware of the fact that they wanted to be here. They wouldn't have come otherwise."

"That doesn't make me feel less guilty about the fact that they were attacked."

Tali understood, so he didn't protest. He and Julian went to work. Most of the assassins were gathered in a group, and since Tali could see a few cuts, he headed toward them. His brother was doing the same thing. Together, they healed cuts and forming bruises, and one impressive gash on Cora's forehead. She still felt hot, probably due to her fire powers, and Tali gave her a wide berth. He liked her, but he wouldn't enjoy being burned to a crisp.

"What now?" Armand asked.

"Now, you shift into that guy," Julian said, pointing to the half-frozen guy Tali had attacked.

Armand wrinkled his nose. "He shot you."

"I don't care what he did. He has to be the second in command, or the guy in charge of this, anyway. He's the one the Family will want to talk to, so you need to be him."

Armand pouted. "Fine. But I don't like it."

"And we're all aware of that. Now, shift."

Julian was bemused by Armand's protests. He knew Armand would do anything to make sure the mission was successful, but it was still hilarious to hear him bitch about it.

Armand shifted into the man on the ground, and it was impressive. Julian had never seen him shift, and even though he knew what Armand could do, it was a shock. He was now identical to the man who'd shot Julian.

Julian cleared his throat and looked at the other people who'd attacked them. A few of them were conscious, and since he needed answers, he went toward them. "I want information," he said as he reached them.

One of them spat on the ground in front of him. "We're not going to tell you anything," he said.

Julian agreed that guy in particular wouldn't, so he turned his attention to the other guy. He looked nervous as he peered at the assassins standing around him, and Julian hoped that meant he'd be able to convince the guy. "What about you? Will you tell me where your boss is?"

"He's going to kill me."

"You think I care or that you're going to make it out of this alive if you don't tell us anything?"

The guy licked his lips. He looked young, too young to be doing this kind of thing. It made Julian want to strangle the head of the Family. "I won't be able to go back if I talk to you."

"Shut your mouth," the other guy snapped. He looked like he wanted to beat up the younger guy, and thankfully, Julian wasn't the only one who noticed it. North grabbed the one who wouldn't talk and dragged him away kicking and screaming, leaving Julian with the young one.

Julian crouched in front of him. "I know this is scary, but I need answers, and I won't stop until I get them. I don't want to hurt you, but I will if I have to."

The guy's eyes were wide. "All right. I'll tell you what you want to know."

"Who's your boss? I know it's not Giovanni, because I killed him a while ago." And while Beck thought his son had taken his place, Julian had to be sure.

"His son Luciano. He took charge after you killed his father."

"And why has he been after me? Because I killed his father?"

"Yes. He wants revenge. He wants to kill you."

Julian's lips twisted into a smile. "And I bet he wants to torture me before doing it."

"Yes. He's been talking about it for a while. I'm sorry."

"As long as you weren't planning on killing me yourself, you don't have a reason to apologize for that." Julian got back to his feet and looked at Roark. "What do you think?"

"I would feel better if we knew where this guy is and if we have to expect him to fight back, as well as how many people he has around." His gaze shifted to the guy on the ground. "Can you answer those questions, too?"

The guy looked like he wanted to say no, but he nodded. "I'll tell you anything you want to know. I'm going to have to run away anyway. The Family will kill me otherwise."

"They won't kill you," Julian said. "They won't be able to, because they'll be trying to get their strength back and rebuild the family. Once I'm done with them, they won't be *the Family* anymore. You don't have to worry about that."

The guy's eyes were wide. "You're going to kill him?"

Julian grinned. "I'm a professional assassin. What did you think I was going to do?" It was a lie, but the kid didn't know that. Julian wasn't actually planning on killing Luciano — if he died, someone else would take his place, and Julian would still be in trouble.

That was enough to get the kid to talk, though. He seemed eager to tell Julian everything he needed to know. That was a good thing. Julian hadn't expected things to be this easy, but he'd been shot, so he supposed it hadn't been.

Once they had all the information they needed from the guy, Julian moved toward Roark. "I don't think we'll get anything else from him," he murmured.

"I agree. But we don't need anything else. We know where Luciano is, how many people he has around, and how secure his place is. We're good to go."

Julian nodded. "I'm ready to leave when you are."

"We're going, then."

Roark gestured at Armand and Dasha to come closer. They'd decided they would be the only ones going. Having Lawrence and Evan in Julian's pockets had been tempting, but there was a possibility someone would pat Julian down, and they couldn't risk it.

As soon as they got there, Roark would make it so that everyone but them had an image of the place without himself and Dasha in it. It was his power—he could create images in people's minds and make them think they were in other places. That wasn't what he was aiming for today, though. He didn't want himself and Dasha to be seen, but Armand in his shifted form and Julian weren't a problem.

They could have shimmered back to the warehouse, but Roark didn't want to leave Julian alone, and Julian was grateful for that. He wasn't afraid, but even though he had all the information he could get, the Family wasn't easy to deal with. It was dangerous, and he wanted to come back to his mate by the end of the day.

"Be careful," Tali murmured as he hugged Julian.

"I will be. And don't come, whatever you feel through the bond. Roark will keep me safe, and I don't want to have to worry about you."

"Easier said than done, but I'll stay away."

That would have to do. Julian understood why Tali was hesitant to promise that, but he needed his mate to stay away.

Julian walked up to Armand, who was bouncing on his feet. They'd decided that Armand would act as if he'd captured Julian and had brought him back. He would do it long enough to get to Luciano. Then, once they were there, he would drop the pretense. Dasha and Roark would be invisible.

Dasha shimmered the four of them in front of a house.

Julian could see all of them, and he hoped Roark was working his magic as Armand opened the door as if he owned the place and dragged him inside.

The place was huge and luxurious. Everything was white and gold, and there were flowers on every table. A chandelier hung from the ceiling, and if this was the entrance, Julian could only imagine what the rest of the house looked like.

"He's in his office?" he asked a man sitting behind a desk in the entrance.

The man stared with wide eyes but nodded. "Yeah. He's waiting for you."

Armand continued dragging Julian around. They knew where to go thanks to the kid, so when they reached a guard standing by a door in an empty hallway, they knew where they were.

"You caught him," the man said.

Armand gave Julian a shake. "Didn't take long, either. He's in?"

"Of course. He's waiting for you. Where are the others?"

"Most of them are still over there, cleaning up."

The man grinned, and Julian had to resist the urge to punch him. He wanted to go back to Tali in one piece, though, so he stayed silent and quiet. The man opened the door, and Armand and Julian walked through it.

Just like the rest of the house, the office was luxurious. Everything Julian could see was white and gold. It made him wrinkle his nose, because who liked gold? Especially when there was so much of it.

"Well, well, well. Julian. Welcome to my home," the man behind the desk said. At least that piece of furniture wasn't gold but a dark wood color.

"You have bad taste when it comes to furniture," Julian told him.

Luciano blinked. "Excuse me?"

"You heard me. You have bad taste." Armand let go of Julian and shifted back. Julian grinned. "Also, your people aren't good at what they do."

Luciano got to his feet, alarmed, but Roark and Dasha were behind him. They both put a hand on his shoulders and pushed him back into his chair. His eyes widened even more. He clearly hadn't expected them to be there, and Julian felt smug.

Luciano looked like his father. He had the same kind of expression, one that said that he thought he was superior to everyone else and that he could do whatever he wanted to them. Julian would make sure he knew it was bullshit.

Julian sat in one of the chairs in front of the desk and raised his feet, putting them on the desk. It was obvious Luciano wanted to tell him to take them off, but he was smart enough not to.

"So, you've been hunting me for a while," Julian said.

"You killed my father. It can't go unpunished."

"See, that's where you're wrong. It *can* go unpunished, and it will. Your father was an asshole, and so are you. But I haven't been hired to kill you, so I won't."

Luciano frowned. "Why are you here, then?"

Julian gestured at Roark and Dasha. "Because of them. See, I knew that even if I killed you, someone else would replace you at the head of the family. This won't stop until the Family is decimated, and honestly, I have better things to do with my life. So here's the deal. You'll leave me alone, and me and my friends won't destroy you and your family."

"You really think I'll agree to that?"

"I know you will . . . because these people around you? They're not just my friends. They're also the council assassins, and I'm sure you've heard of them."

Luciano peeked over his shoulder. Roark grinned at him, and it wasn't a nice smile.

"As you can see, I have the support of the council and their assassins. If you continue coming after me, we'll take care of you, but there won't even be one member left of your family. Is that what you want?"

Luciano stared at Julian. "If I promise to let you go, you'll leave the Family alone?"

"I will, unless, of course, I get hired to kill one of you. But even then, you better stay away. You know you deserve to die in the most painful way. At least I'll make it quick. What do you say?"

Julian stared, hoping the answer would be yes. He had better things to do than to hunt the Family. He wanted to get back to Tali, and he wanted to do it now.

He wouldn't move from here until he got an answer, though.

Tali bit his lower lip, his focus on the bond he shared with Julian. He couldn't feel any pain or fear, and he hoped it was a good thing and that it didn't mean that Julian was unconscious.

He'd wanted to go with Julian and the others, but he hadn't even asked. He'd known what the answer would be, and honestly, it wouldn't have been wrong. He might know how to defend himself, but he wasn't a fighter, and he didn't want to hinder Julian, especially not right now. Julian knew what he was doing, and he wasn't alone. Tali had to believe Roark, Armand, and Dasha would keep him safe.

It was hard. Even though they shared a bond and Tali could feel what Julian felt, it was terrifying not to be able to see him. It was even scarier not to be able to protect him, even though Tali understood how stupid that was. How could he protect Julian? Julian was a professional assassin, while Tali was a healer. Those two things had nothing to do with each other.

Still, Tali was nervous, and he needed to do something.

Since he didn't have anything to do, he moved among the people who had been captured and made sure there was nothing he could do for them. They might be the bad guys, but it didn't mean they shouldn't be healed. By the time he'd healed a few, he was back to the kid who had confessed everything.

Because that was what he was. He had to be in his early twenties, and he looked more like a kid than a man. Tali felt kind of sorry for him, but he also hoped that this experience would put him back on the right track.

He crouched next to him, gesturing at him. "Are you hurt anywhere?" he asked.

The kid's eyes were wide as he shook his head. "I'm fine."

"Are you sure? Because I can heal you."

The kid hesitated. "Why would you? I attacked your people. I'm bad."

Tali snorted. "Sure you are. So? Are you hurt?"

The kid shrugged one shoulder. "Not really. I took a punch to the face, but I'll be fine."

That might be the truth, but Tali still reached for his face. He could feel the bruise forming under his skin, even though nothing was broken. He healed it quickly, then lowered his hand. The kid was still staring at him.

"Seriously. Why are you doing this?" he asked.

"Because I need something to distract myself."

"He's important to you, isn't he?"

Tali didn't have to ask who he was talking about. The kid had seen him and Julian earlier. "He is." Tali was taking a big risk by admitting that, but he didn't think this kid would go back to the Family, not if he was given a chance not to. "Are you going back?"

"I don't think I'll be allowed to. I'll probably end up in jail after this."

"And once you're out?" Because he hadn't actually done anything. As far as Tali was concerned, this kid didn't deserve the same sentence as the others. Even though he'd been there for a specific reason, he'd still helped Julian. He'd told him everything he needed to know, and unless it had been a trick, Tali felt he shouldn't be punished as harshly as the others.

"I don't want to go back," the kid began.

"But?"

"But I don't know if I have a choice. I don't have anyone else."

"What's your name?"

The kid blinked but answered. "Marco."

"Okay. Well, I'm going to give you my phone number. Once you're out of jail, I want you to call me."

"Why?"

"Because I don't think you're a bad guy. I think you didn't have anything else and that you were pulled into this even though you didn't want to. I want to help you get back on your feet."

"I don't understand."

"There's nothing to understand."

Just then, Julian appeared in front of the warehouse. Tali got to his feet, but before leaving, he squeezed Marco's shoulder. "Everything will be all right. Even if you spend some time in jail, you didn't do anything wrong here. You'll be fine."

He left Marco sitting on the ground and rushed toward Julian. Julian turned, and when he saw him, he opened his arms. Tali didn't even hesitate. He threw himself at Julian, wrapping his arms around him, squishing them together until he could barely breathe.

Julian chuckled. "I take it you missed me?"

Tali leaned back and slapped Julian's shoulder. "You're not

funny. I was worried. What happened? What did you do? What did *they* do? Are you hurt?"

Julian chuckled again. He looked more relaxed, and Tali hoped it meant things had gone well. "Slow down. I won't be able to answer if you don't let me speak."

Tali glared at him, but he wasn't angry. "Well? I'm waiting."

Julian looked around. The other assassins had gathered around them, and they were waiting, too. "I threatened the Family. I told Luciano that the council and the council assassins would come after him if he continued hunting me and that as long as he left me alone, we would leave them alone, too, unless we were hired to kill one of them. He agreed to stop. I guess he's afraid of you guys?"

Armand snickered. "Of course he's afraid of us. Look at me. I'm terrifying."

Julian snorted. "Not really, but if it makes you feel better, I think I can quake in my boots every time I see you."

"I think we're done here," Roark said, patting Julian's shoulder. "Everyone, go back home. The enforcers are taking over. Dasha will shimmer all of you." He turned to Dasha. "I'll go back with Jolyn."

Dasha nodded and moved toward the others, and Roark turned his attention back to Julian. "You did a good job."

"Will he be allowed to stay?" Tali asked because he had to know.

Julian grimaced. "Now probably wasn't the right moment to ask that," he told Tali.

Roark interrupted him before he could say anything else. "It won't be a problem. Don't worry about it, Julian. No one is going to kick you out of the council assassins, even though you're not one of us. Besides, I know Win has been talking to the council. I have no doubt they'll see how you behaved in this case and make the right decision."

"And if I never become a council assassin?" Julian asked.

"You'll still be welcome with us. You're Tali's mate. We won't ever ask you to leave, not unless you do something that earns you that. Welcome to the family."

Tali could feel how elated Julian was. He and Roark shook hands, and as soon as they were done, Tali took Julian's face in both his hands and kissing him senseless. "See?" he asked in a whisper. "Everything went well."

"It could have been a disaster," Julian pointed out.

"But it wasn't, and now you don't have to go anywhere. We can go home."

Home wasn't ready yet, but in the meantime, the Gillham pack territory was that for them. While Jolyn and Roark shimmered away, Tali wrapped his arms around his mate and Julian did the same. They appeared in one of the spots still open for them in pack territory, and together, they walked back to the house they were sharing with the others.

It might not be home yet, and it might never be since they wouldn't stay long, but home wasn't merely a place. It was the people waiting for them inside the house. It was the people who had helped them with Julian's problem, who had welcomed him into their fold.

Tali and Julian both had two families, but the one with the council assassins was the most important one for both of them. Tali never wanted to lose any of them, and he was grateful Julian was part of it now, too.

CHAPTER SEVEN

"We should stick around and help. They're going to need it," Tali said.

Julian put his hands on his hips and stared at his mate. "Don't you want to meet my family?"

Tali sighed and sat on one of the chairs in the middle of the hallway. "Of course I want to meet them."

"That's a lie."

"It's not. I do want to meet your family. I'm just afraid."

Julian wasn't surprised. He could feel it through the bond, but he'd learned to ask Tali how he was feeling rather than assume. "They'll love you," he told his mate.

"That doesn't help as much as I wish it did. I know my family loves you, but it's not the same."

Julian crouched in front of his mate and took his hands in his. "Tali. Look at me."

Tali looked up. "What?"

"We can stay and help the others fix the warehouse. I can call my parents and tell them something came up. But I'd really like for you to meet them. I know that you might be intimidated because my parents and my sister are professional assassins, but I promise you, they won't hurt you."

Tali snorted. "Why would I think they'd hurt me? I don't care that they're professional assassins, although I have to point out that you told me your mother was retired. I live with professional assassins every day. That's not my problem."

Julian should have realized that, but still. He knew his parents could be intimidating. "What is it, then?"

112

Tali sighed and linked their fingers together. "I don't know. I guess I'm a bit scared that they won't like me. What will happen then? Will they ask you to choose between the two of us?"

"Of course not. Even if they hate you, they won't do that to me. They know you're my mate and that we're bonded."

"That's not reassuring, though. They're going to have to tolerate me even if they hate me?"

Julian didn't know how to deal with this. "They *won't* hate you." He was sure of that. "I promise. They're happy that you make me happy, and that's all there is to it."

Tali sighed again. "Fine. We can go."

"And once we're back home, I promise we can cuddle on our bed," Julian said.

That finally got Tali to smile. "Will you be in your rabbit form?"

"If you want me to be."

"As if you don't want me to scratch under your chin."

Julian did. He hadn't had anyone to cuddle him in his rabbit form since he'd left his family. It was intimate, and not anything he could allow anyone but his mate and the people he was closest with to do. For now, it was something he reserved for Tali, although he suspected that wouldn't last for much longer. The last time Armand had walked in on him—and yes, it had happened several times because Armand didn't knock on doors—he'd squealed and had grabbed Julian from Tali's hands. Julian had been angry and he'd almost bitten him, but Armand had started rubbing his head, and Julian had given in.

No matter how crazy they were, the council assassins were his family, and he had to accept them the way they were, including Armand.

He offered Tali his hand. "Come on. Let's go."

Tali took it, and Julian pulled him to his feet.

They walked through the new warehouse. All of the council assassins were there, moving furniture around and settling down in the private and common spaces. It would take more than a few days for them to feel at home, but Julian knew it would happen eventually. This warehouse was much bigger than the older one, probably because the council assassins' family was growing so much. They were adding mates to the mix, and it made it even more like a family. The warehouse would be their home, and they wanted everything to be perfect.

"Already slacking?" Roark asked, passing by them carrying a chair.

"We're meeting my family," Julian said.

Roark arched a brow. "The professional assassins?"

"They won't kill Tali. Don't worry."

"I know they won't. They'd have to deal with me if they do."

"And with me. But I love him. They will, too."

Roark's gaze softened. "I'm sure you're right."

Julian could still feel the nervousness coursing through the bond he shared with Tali, but he knew that nothing would soothe Tali better than actually meeting his family. He already knew they would love him. The only way to show that to Tali was to introduce them.

They headed toward the shimmering room, and Tali took out his phone. He opened the app Beck had designed, entered the code, then shimmered them out.

He'd been focused on Julian's thoughts, so they landed at the front door of the house in which Julian's parents lived. They had a few moments of respite before anyone noticed they were there, and Julian turned to his mate. "If you're too uncomfortable, we can leave at any time."

"I can do this," Tali said, standing taller. "Besides, I really want that cuddling."

"I know you can." Julian leaned to kiss him, and just as their lips brushed, the front door swung open.

Julian turned to look at his mother. "Hi, Mom."

She ignored him, focusing on Tali. "You look adorable." She grabbed Tali's arm and pulled him into a hug. "I'm so happy to meet you."

Tali looked at Julian with wide eyes, but Julian shrugged. The only thing to do was to power through it.

Julian's mom dragged Tali inside to the kitchen, where the rest of the family was gathered. "I'm Augusta, but you can call me Mom if you want, or not if you don't want to. Whatever you're comfortable with. This is my husband, Rob. Then, there's Kara, Julian's sister, and of course, Sam."

Sam rolled his eyes. "I wonder why I'm always the last one."

"That's because you're the black sheep of the family," Kara said, bumping their shoulders together.

She got to her feet and headed toward Tali, hugging him more gently than their mother had. "Welcome to the family," she told him." She leaned away. "You're way too gorgeous for my brother."

Julian huffed, but his heart felt like it was about to explode. He'd known his family would welcome Tali, but this was even better than what he'd expected.

Julian's father and Sam were a bit more careful, but they still shook Tali's hand and talked to him. Tali looked overwhelmed, and Julian was grateful when the family turned back to him. They already knew what had happened in the past weeks, and while they were angry at him for not coming to them, they also agreed he'd done the right thing.

Dinner went perfectly, and Julian knew he and Tali would fit in here just as well as they fit with the council assassins. The entire family teased Sam for not following in their footsteps, but Sam was used to it, and he answered in the same tone, pointing out that he wasn't the only one now that Tali was part of the family—although Kara didn't agree since Tali lived with the council assassins. Tali stayed mostly silent, but Julian could feel that he was happy, and that was all he needed.

Julian got them out of there as soon as possible, brushing off his mother's questions and demands. "I promise we'll be back soon, but we're still moving in, so we have to go back," he told her.

She didn't look convinced. "As long as you're not hiding anything else."

"I promise I'm not. I was only trying to keep you guys safe."

"Maybe so, but we don't need you to. We're perfectly fine, and we could have held our own against the Family. I have half a mind to go there and kick Clemente's ass."

"Please don't. He promised he would stay away from me, and I think he will. I don't need you to fight my battles, Mom."

"All right. But if there's anything, call us. We'll be there for you."

"I know." Julian had always known it.

He was relieved when he and Tali were able to shimmer home. The noises in the new warehouse had quieted down as people drifted to their respective bedrooms. They'd all decided to stay, even though the warehouse was still a bit of a mess. It looked a bit like they were camping, but everyone was in their bedroom. They needed time, which was what Julian and Tali needed, too. Julian pulled Tali toward their bedroom, and as he closed the door behind them, he relaxed. This was a safe haven, a place in which they could close the world out and just be together.

Tali turned to look at him, "So? Are you shifting?"

Julian laughed. "From your words, it's almost as if you

love me only because I'm a rabbit shifter."

Tali's eyes twinkled. "Well, that's a big plus. But no. I love you because you're you, Julian. I love all of you, not just your rabbit form."

Julian stepped closer. "And I love you." He really did.

He loved everything about Tali and their new life together. He couldn't believe he had it, not after everything he'd gone through. He still wasn't sure he would be allowed to become a council assassin, but even if he couldn't, he had what he'd been yearning for — a mate, a big family, a place in which he could be himself.

You may also enjoy the following from eXtasy Books Inc:

The Only Right Choice
Catherine Lievens

Excerpt

"Dan and I will talk in my office," Jerome, the fox alpha, said. He stared at Chris and Gwen, his daughter.

When Chris and his father had arrived at the alpha's house, he and his daughter had been waiting. Chris didn't understand why she was here, but he hadn't asked. He didn't want to make anyone uncomfortable, and he knew how to behave when he was with other alphas. Still, he'd thought his father had wanted him there to include him at the meeting, not to leave him with Jerome's daughter.

He looked at his father, but his dad was looking away as if avoiding his gaze. It was strange, and Chris would make sure to ask him about it once they were back in the car. In the meantime, he could wait in the living room with Gwen. They didn't know each other, but they were about the same age, so they could probably find something to talk about.

"Of course, Dad," Gwen said. She looked down, the perfect image of the submissive daughter.

Chris didn't like it. His sisters had never behaved like that with their father. He was their alpha, but more importantly, he was their dad, and they'd always talked back to him and told him what they thought about his orders. Gwen didn't seem to have the same fire in her, and it made Chris wonder how she'd been raised and what kind of father Jerome was.

She was pretty. Even though Chris was very much gay and in love with Jacob, he could see that. Her long blond hair was braided, with wisps escaping from it and framing her face. Her cheeks were pink and her blue eyes glittered. Any other guy would have been all over her.

Jerome blinked at her. "All right. We'll go to the office, then," he said. He exchanged a glance with Chris's father before they both disappeared down the hallway.

Chris looked around the living room. He supposed he and Gwen could watch TV or something like that.

They both heard the office door close in the distance, and Gwen's demeanor changed. She went from submissive to standing tall and glaring at Chris, and Chris didn't understand what was happening.

"I am not marrying you," she snapped.

Chris had no idea what she was talking about. "Good. Because I haven't asked you to marry me." And he wasn't going to. He and Jacob had broken up, but it was too soon, and besides, he was only nineteen.

Gwen crossed her arms over her chest. "That's why you're here, though. You want to marry me. You want to unite the fox and the bobcats."

"I have no idea what you're talking about. I swear." But he didn't like the sound of it.

"Why should I believe you?"

Chris hesitated, but he knew the best way for her to believe him was to tell her about Jacob. "Because I'm in love with someone else. We broke up, and I know there's no going back, but I still have feelings for him, and I can't think of marrying anyone else right now. Why do you think I want to marry you?"

Gwen looked like she wanted to ask more about Jacob, but instead, she dropped her arms. "Because my father asked me to consider it. Your father didn't?"

"No." Hell, he'd been talking about Jacob in the car as they came here. "Can you tell me what happened?"

"Nothing much." She huffed and flopped onto the couch. She looked nothing like the submissive woman she'd been only minutes ago. "My father came to me yesterday. He said he wanted to talk, and when I agreed to listen to him, he explained that he wanted me to consider marrying you. He talked about you, told me that you're nineteen, the future alpha, and that it would be good both for the clowder and the skulk to be united. I don't want that, though. I don't know why my brother can't marry one of your sisters. He's the alpha heir, not me."

"Probably because they're already married." Chris sat on the edge of the couch, giving Gwen space. He was angry at his father. He couldn't believe he was doing this right after asking about Jacob. He'd acknowledged how much Chris loved Jacob, yet he'd turned around and had suggested a wedding. Hell, he hadn't even talked to Chris about it. He'd left that to Gwen, and Chris would make sure he knew what he thought about this once they were back in the car.

"So you're not okay with this?" Gwen asked.

"I'm not. Even if I wasn't in love with someone else, I'm only nineteen, and you're what? The same age?"

"Eighteen. And yes, that's way too young to get married."

"I understand why our fathers want to unite the clowder and the skulk, but I don't think it's a good idea to do it this way."

"You're right. Even if I had agreed to marry you, I don't want to get married to someone who's in love with someone else. No offense, but I don't want to get married just to make sure the skulk is okay. I deserve more."

"I agree."

Gwen sat up, crossing her legs under herself. "Do you want

to talk about the guy? The one you're in love with?"

"Not really."

"You said you broke up with him," Gwen said, ignoring what Chris had just said.

Chris sighed. This was going to be a long meeting, and he knew Gwen would stay with him the entire time. "We did. But I don't want to talk about it."

Gwen shrugged. "Pity because I don't have anything else to do. Come on. Tell me his name."

Chris could have kissed his father when he heard him and Jerome come down the hallway about an hour later. Gwen had tried to get details about Chris's relationship with Jacob the entire time, and Chris had had a hard time denying her. He might have talked to her if they'd been friends, but they weren't. He didn't know Gwen, even though their fathers thought they should get married. He doubted he would ever see her again, unless their fathers insisted. He was pretty sure his dad wouldn't, though, not after Chris was done with him.

Chris got to his feet, nodding when his dad and Jerome walked into the room. They both looked on edge, probably expecting Chris and Gwen to say something about the situation they'd been dumped in.

Chris only narrowed his eyes at his father. His father sighed heavily, then turned to Jerome. "Well, we're going to head out. I'll call you once I know more."

"You do that." Jerome looked from Chris to Gwen. "Everything okay while we were gone?"

"Of course," Chris said. Gwen was back at playing submissive, and she was looking away. Chris could see her vibrating with anger, though, and he suspected her father would be yelled at as soon as he and his dad were gone.

He felt quite smug at the idea.

He waited until he and his father were back in the car to turn to him. "I can't believe you did that to me."

His dad sighed again. "I'm sorry. I should have explained why we were coming, but I knew you would refuse if I told you about it."

"And you know exactly why. I can't believe you asked me about Jacob only to throw me in Gwen's arms ten minutes later. You know I'm still in love with him." The words made Chris choke, but he had to say them. "Look, I realize that me and Jacob can never be together. It's the reason I came back home. I knew there was no hope. It doesn't mean you have to push me toward someone else, though. I'm not ready for another relationship, and I'm nowhere near ready to get married. I'm only nineteen, and I'm still trying to learn everything I need to know to take your place when you retire. Don't force this on to me, too."

"Is that what I did? Force the alpha position onto you?"

Chris couldn't answer that. He pressed his lips together and shook his head. "That's not what I'm talking about right now. Promise me you won't try to arrange another marriage for me. Even if you want me to marry someone for the good of the clowder, I want a say in it. I don't want it to be a secret or a surprise."

His father peered at him before turning his attention back to the road. "Fine. I promise I won't do it again."

Chris leaned in his seat and looked out the window. It was a victory, albeit a tiny one. He'd sorely needed it, and he was relieved he wouldn't have to see Gwen again, not like this anyway.

It didn't solve any of his other problems, but it was a start, or at least, he hoped so.

"See you tomorrow," Thomas said as he closed his front door.

Jacob smiled at him, then turned around to head to his truck. His day was over, and he was headed home to have dinner and relax.

Except he didn't want to go home.

His house didn't feel like home anymore. He'd spent so much time at the Bishop house with everyone else that it felt more like home than his own house. He didn't understand why, yet he did. The Bishop house was the place in which he'd fallen in love with Chris. It was the place in which they'd been together. It was also the place in which Jacob had friends. All the carriers except a few ones had been friendly, and even though they weren't best friends, they were still part of Jacob's family now. A lot of them had left, but five were still there, and Jacob decided to head over to them rather than go home to an empty house. He could have dinner with them, talk, and make sure they were okay. It had to be a big change for them to be almost alone in a big house after sharing it with so many people. It was emptier than it had been but still fuller than Jacob's place was.

He drove to the Bishop house, smiling when he saw the lights on inside the house. There were only five carriers left, but they weren't alone. A few guards were still there, too, and they always ate with the carriers. They were like a big family, and just being here made Jacob feel better.

He couldn't have Chris back, but this, he could have.

He turned the engine off and rushed out of the truck, climbing the porch steps two by two. He knocked on the door, and he heard the conversation in the kitchen stop before someone moved to open the door.

He beamed when Hector opened. Hector blinked, clearly surprised to see him, but he stepped aside to let him in. "We didn't expect you."

"Do you want me to leave?" Jacob asked because he would never force his company on anyone.

Hector laughed and shook his head. "Of course not. You're part of the family. Come in. You're just in time for dinner, but then, I suspect that's why you're here."

"You're right. I didn't want to cook tonight."

"I see."

Jacob suspected Hector knew why he was here and that it wasn't because he didn't want to cook, but thankfully, he didn't say anything about it. Instead, he led the way to the kitchen, where the other four carriers and the two guards were sitting and cooking. Jacob nodded at Gail and Darrel, the guards, and sat at the counter with them, Burnell, and Lennox. Redley, Hector, and Turner were cooking.

Jacob relaxed. It was familiar. It was family.

"We didn't expect you," Redley said. He was using a wooden spoon to mix something in a pot.

"I just finished work, and I was too tired to cook," Jacob said, using the same excuse he'd used before.

"Well, you're always welcome here. All of you are. We're grateful you're allowing us to stay in this house, and we want to make life easier for you if it's at all possible."

"You don't have to do that. You know you're welcome to stay for as long as you want regardless of what you do."

Redley grinned. "Careful. I might decide to stay for the rest of my life."

"That wouldn't be a problem. You can stay if you want. Thomas was clear." But Jacob wondered why Redley hadn't gone home. He was a fox shifter. The clowder was safe for carriers now, and Nico and Chris had gone. Redley was still here, though. "I'm surprised you stayed," Jacob said. It might not be the right moment to ask, but everyone here had learned to be honest with each other. It was the only way they'd managed to make it work with so many people living together.

Redley sighed. "I don't know. I don't hate the clowder or anything like that. I just never felt like it was home, you know? Everyone there knew I was a carrier, and they treated me differently for it."

"Do they treat Jacob and Chris differently, too?" Lennox asked.

"Not really. But then, they're the alpha's sons. Chris is going to be the next alpha. I'm no one. I'm just a carrier, and it showed. I'd rather not go back to that if I have a choice."

"Well, you do. You can stay here," Jacob told him.

Redley smiled. "And I'm grateful for that. Truly. The clowder has never felt like home, but this place does. I'm grateful for everything the cete did for me."

"Don't even mention it." The cete had done what they had to do, what anyone else would have done in their place. They'd had a safe place for the carriers, and they'd made sure none of them got hurt. They'd helped those who had been imprisoned, and now, they were free.

"Have you heard about Chris?" Hector asked.

Jacob could have sworn everyone in the room winced at his words. "I haven't. He hasn't called me, and I'm not going to call him," Jacob told him.

Hector bit his lower lip. "Look, I know everyone is walking on eggshells around you when it comes to this, but I have to say it. I think it's a pity the two of you broke up."

"I agree. It is."

"But it's not going to make a difference, is it?"

Jacob sighed. He didn't want to talk about Chris, but he understood why the others were asking. His and Chris's fights had been loud, so everyone knew why Chris had left without Jacob, and why things couldn't work between them. Jacob wasn't surprised they were asking, though. They had hope, just like Jacob had had in the beginning. "He needs an alpha mate. That's not me. It can never be me."

"Pity. You would have been a good alpha mate."

Jacob snorted. "I doubt that. I'm way too selfish to be an alpha mate." Which was why he'd been with Christ even though he'd known things wouldn't work. He'd hoped Chris would leave his clowder and the alpha position, but of course, he'd been wrong.

"Well, even though you don't have him, you have us," Turner said. "It's not the same thing, but we're still family, aren't we?"

Jacob forced himself to smile at him and nodded. "We are."

Turner was a skunk shifter. Even though things were getting better for most of the shifters in the forest, some groups resisted change, and the skunks were one of those. Turner still didn't feel comfortable enough to go home. That was fine with Jacob, and with everyone else. The Bishop house was these men's home now, and that would never change.

It was also Jacob's, but he knew that would have to change. He had a house. Eventually, he would have to stop coming to the Bishop house so often. The five men who lived here deserved to learn to live on their own, and that wouldn't happen if Jacob was always around. In the meantime, though, Jacob was going to do his best to make them see they were welcome in the cete for however long they wanted to stay. No one expected them to leave or to do anything. They could be themselves in a way they couldn't have been if they'd go back home. Hell, for a few of them, it would be too dangerous to go back.

But they didn't have to. They had a home and a family, something they'd never had before, and the same went for Jacob. It complicated things, but Jacob wouldn't change it for anything in the world.

ABOUT THE AUTHOR

Catherine is the creator of several series, most of them paranormal, including the Whitedell Pride Series and the Gillham Pack Series. While she graduated in translation, she decided to go the writer's way because it was more fun to create her own stories and characters.

She's been living in Italy for more than twenty years, but she's a daughter of the North—Belgium to be precise—and she misses it so much that she's already planning to move back.

She loves pizza—probably too much—her son, her pets, and of course, books. She sneaks some reading time into her schedule every time she has five minutes free from writing, demands from her various pets and son, and lastly, housework.

Connect with her:

lievens.catherine@gmail.com
BookBub: https://www.bookbub.com/authors/catherine-lievens
Website: https://authorcatherinelievens.com/
Facebook: https://www.facebook.com/catherine.lievens.9
Facebook Group: https://www.facebook.com/groups/411788002341528/
Twitter: https://twitter.com/authorCLievens
Newsletter: http://eepurl.com/c-uvKn

www.ingramcontent.com/pod-product-compliance
Lightning Source LLC
Chambersburg PA
CBHW060630130626
46555CB00002B/733